ATTITUDE

ESPECIALLY FOR GIRLS® Presents

ATTITUDE

THE PORTRAITS COLLECTION™

Marilyn Kaye

FAWCETT GIRLS ONLY • NEW YORK

RLI: $\dfrac{\text{VL 6 \& up}}{\text{IL 8 \& up}}$

A Fawcett Girls Only Book
Published by Ballantine Books

Copyright © 1990 by Daniel Weiss Associates, Inc.

Library of Congress Catalog Card Number: 90-92914

ISBN 0-449-14605-7

Manufactured in the United States of America

First Edition: July 1990

For George and Florence Rudman,
with love.

1

LINDSAY CRAWFORD SAT CROSS-LEGGED ON A TWIN bed in her best friend's room. A bottle of nail polish was balanced on her knee. As she stroked the color over her nails, she grinned at Jennifer, who was sitting on the opposite bed, talking on the telephone.

"Look, we made our decision, and it's final!" Jennifer said. "If you don't like it, write up a complaint and stick it in the student council box, okay? Bye!"

She slammed down the receiver and flopped back on her bed with a groan.

"What is it this time?" Lindsay asked.

"Someone complaining because the art magazine got fifty dollars more in the budget than the literary magazine. Why do they have to bother *me* with this stuff?"

"Because you're vice president of the student council, and it's your job."

"I know . . . I know. I'm just wondering why I

ever decided to run for office. Am I a glutton for punishment or something?"

"No." Lindsay carefully screwed the polish cap back on the bottle. "You're just a sucker for causes."

"You may have a point," Jennifer noted ruefully. "I guess apathy has its benefits."

"What do you think of this color?" Lindsay thrust her hands toward Jennifer for inspection.

"It's too purple."

Lindsay blew on her nails. "*I* like it."

"Then why'd you bother to ask my opinion?"

"Just curious. I wanted to make sure you still have crummy taste."

Jennifer picked up her pillow.

"Don't you dare throw that!" Lindsay shrieked. "You'll ruin my nails!"

"Girls!" Mrs. Gold stood in the doorway, shaking her head. "You two never change."

Lindsay grinned at Jennifer's mother. "You mean we still act like little kids?" she asked.

She and Jennifer had met the first day of kindergarten. They couldn't have been more different. Jennifer looked like a tomboy in her blue jeans and T-shirt, her red curly hair tied back in an untidy pony tail. Lindsay was the perfect little girl in a freshly ironed dress with a ribbon in her hair. Jennifer was talkative and outspoken. Lindsay was quiet and shy. Maybe they had been drawn together because they admired each other's differences.

Whatever the reason was, the bond between them had formed almost instantly. Discovering that they both lived in the same high-rise apartment building cemented the relationship. They'd been best friends ever since. For eleven years they'd traded secrets, gossiped, argued, and seen each other through good and bad times.

Really bad times. Like a year ago, when out of the blue, Lindsay's life had been shattered. Thinking of it, Lindsay felt the all-too-familiar dark cloud descending upon her and had to force herself to keep smiling.

"Jennifer, what happened to your skirt?" Mrs. Gold asked.

"A cab splashed me on the way home from school. Is it my fault New York is filthy?"

"I'm going to the dry cleaner's later. Be sure to give me your skirt before I go. In the meantime I have to get back to the kitchen."

"What are you making?" Jennifer asked.

"Brownies. Want to taste-test my new recipe?"

Jennifer and Lindsay grinned at each other. "Sure," Lindsay said. They followed Mrs. Gold to the kitchen, where she took the tray of brownies out of the oven and set them down on the kitchen counter. Being careful not to smear her nails, Lindsay picked one up. So did Jennifer.

Lindsay took a bite. "Mmm, these are fantastic. What's in them?"

"Caramel and coconut and chocolate chips," Mrs. Gold said.

Jennifer looked down at the brownie in her hand and made a face. "That sounds almost disgusting!"

"Then don't eat it," her mother replied.

"What else smells so good?" Lindsay asked.

"Beef Stroganoff," Mrs. Gold smiled. "Would you like to stay for dinner?"

"Thanks, but I can't," Lindsay said. "I've got a date."

Jennifer ate the last of her brownie. "Going out with Parker?"

Lindsay nodded. "Who else?"

"Good grief, look at the time," Mrs. Gold said. "Jen, go take that skirt off. I have to get to the dry cleaner's before they close."

As Jennifer ran out of the kitchen, Mrs. Gold sat back and turned to Lindsay. "Is Parker taking you out to dinner?"

"Yes, luckily. There's never anything to eat at home. I mean, nothing like Beef Stroganoff."

Mrs. Gold smiled. "Your aunt doesn't cook very much, does she?"

"No, cooking isn't exactly Margaret's thing."

Mrs. Gold looked up as the apartment door clicked open in the other room. Moments later Mr. Gold came into the kitchen.

"I'm home," he announced unnecessarily. "How're my lovely wife and daughter?" He peered closely at Lindsay. "Wait, you're not my daughter. Who are you? Where am I?"

Lindsay grinned. "Hi, Mr. Gold."

"Hi, Dad," Jennifer returned to the kitchen in jeans and a T-shirt and handed her mother the crumpled skirt.

With a deep sigh, Mrs. Gold shook out the skirt and folded it neatly. "Dinner's in an hour," she informed Mr. Gold.

"I don't know if I can hold out that long." He

reached for a brownie. Mrs. Gold lightly slapped his hand.

"These are for dessert!" she said sternly. "Now go change for dinner!"

Mr. Gold saluted her. "Yes, ma'am." He winked at Lindsay and left the kitchen.

Mrs. Gold got up. "Okay, I'm going. See you later, Lindsay."

When she and Jennifer were alone again, Lindsay leaned back in her chair and reached for another brownie. She knew she ought to go home and start getting ready for her date, but she didn't really feel like leaving. She dreaded going home and trying to make conversation with her aunt, and she didn't want to leave the Gold's warm, comfortable kitchen.

"Let's get to the important stuff," Jennifer said, breaking the silence. "What are you going to wear tonight?"

"I don't know. I'm trying to think of some outfit Parker hasn't seen yet. It's not easy when you've been going out with someone for two months."

"I wouldn't know," Jennifer said, a little wistfully.

"I offered to ask Parker to fix you up with one of his friends."

"I know," Jennifer said. "I just don't think Parker's friends are my type."

"What's that supposed to mean?"

"No offense," Jennifer said quickly. "It's just that those social register types make me uncomfortable."

"You're not exactly eating in a soup kitchen."

"No, but I'm not exactly in Parker Holland's league, either."

Jennifer had a point. There were basically three groups at Benedict Academy. There was the in crowd—really rich kids whose parents always had their names in society columns and gave huge sums of money to the ballet and opera. Then there were the regular people, like Jennifer and Lindsay; and last, there was a handful of kids on scholarships. Since everyone wore uniforms at Benedict they all looked pretty much the same. But somehow you always knew exactly who was in which group.

"Okay, so Parker's rich. You can't hold that against him."

"No," Jennifer said, looking away. "You can't."

There was a moment of silence. "Jen . . ."

"What?"

"You don't like Parker, do you?"

"What makes you think that?"

"Don't give me that look! I've known you for ten years. Every time I mention his name you look like you've just eaten a lemon."

Jennifer grimaced.

"See! Like that!"

Jennifer picked at the brownie crumb on her plate. "I don't really dislike him," she said slowly. "After all, he's never done anything to me. I just don't get what you see in him."

"You've got to admit he's cute."

"Sure. Parker's good-looking. But what else?"

Lindsay stuttered, "He—he's got charm. And he

treats me really nicely. He's not wild, he doesn't do drugs. . . ."

"And he's very rich."

"Jen-nifer, that's got nothing to do with it!" But when she looked into Jennifer's eyes, Lindsay couldn't help blushing. "Okay, I'll admit it's nice to have a guy pick up the tab sometimes. But I'd go out with Parker even if he didn't have any money."

"Is he intelligent, fun to talk to?"

"Well, he's no intellectual giant. But he's not *stupid*, either." Lindsay broke off and stared at Jennifer. "So that's what's bothering you, huh? You think Parker's superficial, right? Just a conceited, good-looking, shallow preppy."

"Don't get defensive!" Jennifer exclaimed. "I never said that. Look, I've got nothing against Parker. I just think you could do better."

Better than Parker Holland, one of the most popular guys at school? Lindsay didn't think so. She'd seen the looks of envy from girls at school when she walked down the hall with him. Parker was definitely in the very desirable class. Being with him gave Lindsay a secure feeling, a feeling that she had a place where she belonged and was needed, but she didn't know how to explain that to Jennifer.

"Sure I could," she said.

"Are you in love with him?" Jennifer asked.

Lindsay sighed. "I don't know. I like him. How do you know when you're in love anyway?"

"Do you get shivers and chills up and down your spine every time he looks into your eyes?"

"Oh, Jen, you've been reading too many ro-

mances. This is real life. I don't know why you're
so down on Parker. You barely know him."

"I'm sorry," Jennifer said quickly. "You're right.
What are you guys doing tonight, anyway?"

"We're going for Chinese." Lindsay paused. "Actually, we're double-dating with Claire Magnuson
and Ron James."

"Claire Magnuson?" Jennifer put her hand on her
heart. "Ooh, I'm impressed." Lindsay knew what
she meant. A future debutante and president of the
Benedict League, a select girls' society, Claire Magnuson was definitely a force to be reckoned with.
Everyone knew Claire. She was the crème de la
crème of Benedict Academy.

"What does your aunt think of Parker?" Jennifer
couldn't seem to get off the topic.

Lindsay shrugged. "I don't know. She's never
talked about him. I don't think they've ever said
more than two words to each other."

Jennifer looked thoughtful.

"What's up, Jen?"

"I was just wondering what your parents would
have thought of him."

Lindsay stood up. "I have to go," she said
quickly.

"I'm sorry, Lin. I didn't mean—"

"It's okay. Really. I have to take a bath and figure out what I'm going to wear. I'm sure Claire will
look fabulous as usual. I should at least make an
effort."

Jennifer stood up and walked her to the door.
She looked so apologetic, Lindsay forgave her.

"Listen," Lindsay said impulsively. "Do you want

to come to dinner tomorrow night? My aunt was asking me why I never have any friends over."

"Tomorrow night? Saturday? Aren't you going out with Parker?"

"Well, I thought I'd invite him, too. It would be a chance for you to get to know him better."

"Sure," Jennifer said. "That'd be great."

"Perfect," Lindsay said. "Jen, I really want you to like him."

Jennifer's face softened. "Listen, if you're crazy about him, that's all that counts."

Crazy about him wasn't exactly how Lindsay would describe it. He suited her, but again it occurred to her that Jennifer wouldn't understand that, so she didn't bother to explain.

"Yeah, I guess," she said out loud. "I'll call you tomorrow and let you know what time."

"Okay. Have fun tonight."

"I'll try."

Out in the hall Lindsay hit the elevator button and did what she had done since she was a little girl—started counting. When the elevator didn't come by the time she reached ten—which it hardly ever did—she walked over to the stairs and down the three flights to her own apartment.

2

"**M**ARGARET?" LINDSAY CALLED AS SHE STEPPED IN-side the foyer to her own apartment.

There was no response. Lindsay tiptoed into the living room and flicked on the light. The room was bathed in the warm glow of a small chandelier suspended from the ceiling.

She looked around. The room wasn't particu-larly fancy or elegant, but Lindsay loved it any-way. Her father's hobby had been restoring old furniture, and the sofa and gleaming walnut chairs and tables were evidence of his talent. Her moth-er's touches were all over the room, too, mostly souvenirs of the Crawfords' extensive travels. There was a colorful Mexican wall hanging, a col-lection of hand-painted china plates, and an enor-mous porcelain vase overflowing with bright silk flowers.

As Lindsay's gaze swept the room, it settled on the paintings on the wall above the fireplace—a still life, a landscape . . . and the portrait. Lindsay usually was careful to avert her eyes from that particular picture. But this time she moved closer and forced herself to look at it head-on. There they were—Anne Crawford on a small gilt chair, John Crawford standing behind her, one hand lightly resting on her shoulder. Curled up in front of her mother was Lindsay, age eight.

She felt the familiar stinging sensation behind her eyes. She turned away, went to the window, and pressed her face against the glass. In the distance she could see that the treetops in Central Park were a blur of red and gold. Autumn in New York. It used to be her favorite time of the year. But it had been a day like this, a perfect autumn day one year ago, when she'd gotten the call.

She'd been staying up at Jennifer's while her parents were abroad. She wouldn't have even been in her family's apartment except that she wanted a certain sweater to wear that evening. In her mind she could still see herself, clutching the red cashmere sweater and coming down the hall, when the phone rang. She had gone into the kitchen and picked up the receiver.

A woman spoke on the other end, a total stranger; from the embassy, she said. She was calling to tell Lindsay about an accident, a gas leak in a hotel in a city halfway across the world.

It was the kind of story you might find buried in the back of the newspaper or reported toward the end of the news broadcast. If you read it or heard about it, you might feel a distant passing sympathy for the victims. Or, if you had other things on your mind, you might not pay any attention to it at all.

Unless your parents happened to be staying in that hotel.

The days that followed were still fuzzy and out of focus. Time had not made Lindsay's memory any sharper. She could vaguely recall friends and neighbors drifting in and out of the Golds' apartment bearing cakes and flowers. Other images flashed through her mind: the funeral home, a long black limousine, the cemetery in Connecticut in her father's hometown. . . . None of it had seemed real at the time. It still didn't.

What Lindsay did remember clearly was the scene in her parents' lawyer's office a few weeks later. Mr. Morton had been a friend of her parents, and he spoke kindly. "According to the terms of your parents' will, in the event of their . . . decease, custody of the minor child . . ." He peered over his funny, old-fashioned glasses. "That's you, my dear. Custody is granted to the next of kin: Margaret Crawford, sister of John Crawford."

Aunt Margaret? Lindsay had an indistinct recollection of an Aunt Margaret—a slight, shadowy figure from her childhood. She had visited a few times, but she'd never stayed long. She was always just passing through, always in a hurry to get somewhere else. She was at least ten years younger than Lindsay's father—a free-lance writer, Lindsay remembered. Her father had once told her that they'd never been particularly close. Aunt Margaret's last visit had been years ago, when Lindsay was ten. Now this woman she barely remembered would be living with her.

Mr. Morton was still talking. "Unfortunately

we're having some difficulty locating your aunt," he said. "Apparently she's in South America on a writing assignment, and we've been unable to ascertain her exact location. However, we have employed an investigative agency to look into this. I'm sure we'll find her soon."

"You don't have to rush," Lindsay said. "Mrs. Gold says I can stay with them as long as I want."

"Yes, I'm aware of that," Mr. Morton replied. "In fact, the Golds have offered to have you permanently, should your aunt, um, refuse her guardianship."

Lindsay's heart quickened at those words. The Golds were almost a second family to her. She found herself secretly hoping that Aunt Margaret would never be found.

For a while, it had seemed as if Lindsay might get her wish. It was eight months before Margaret Crawford was located. She had been traveling around the mountains of Peru, interviewing the Indians who lived there, for a book she was writing. She moved from village to village. When the investigators finally caught up with her, Aunt Margaret had flown to New York immediately.

Lindsay could still remember every moment of the day when Margaret had first moved into the apartment and become her guardian. Lindsay was dressed up in her best clothes, waiting with Jennifer and Mrs. Gold for her aunt to arrive. As she looked out the windows at the street below, she felt a twinge of excitement. Maybe her aunt would become a friend, a confidante, as Lindsay's mother had been. Or perhaps she would be like Lindsay's father—always cracking jokes and telling funny stories.

But as soon as the intercom buzzed and Lindsay heard her aunt's voice on the other side, she felt sadder than she'd ever before felt in her life. And when she opened the door and saw Margaret standing there in her drab blue suit, surrounded by overstuffed bags, Lindsay knew that her hopes had been completely, totally, futile. Her aunt was nothing like either of her parents, and never would be.

As Lindsay daydreamed, the apartment door clicked open. Lindsay turned.

From her place in the living room, Lindsay watched her slender, brown-haired aunt flip through the mail on the little table next to the door. Margaret's shapeless, olive green dress made her skin look almost sallow. Her bangs fell untidily over the rim of her glasses. *I wish she'd get a haircut*, Lindsay thought.

"Anything for me?" she said out loud.

Margaret jumped. "Oh, Lindsay, you startled me!" She looked back at the mail. "Afraid not." Her smile revealed her slightly crooked front teeth.

Lindsay knew it was ungrateful to be so critical of her aunt, but she couldn't help it. Dull-looking, serious Aunt Margaret was so different from her mother, who'd always been so lighthearted and looked so well put-together in her bright silk dresses and carefully chosen jewelry.

"What time is it?" Margaret asked.

Lindsay looked pointedly at the watch on Margaret's wrist. Margaret's eyes followed hers, and she laughed. "Unbelievable! I actually remembered to put it on this morning! Gosh, it's almost seven. No wonder I'm starving."

Lindsay followed her into the kitchen. Margaret opened the door of the refrigerator. "Unfortunately I did forget to stop at the supermarket. Looks like I'll be ordering Chinese again." Margaret turned to Lindsay. "How about you?"

"I'm going out."

"That's nice."

Funny—it was the little exchanges like this that always brought home to Lindsay how much her life had changed. If she'd told her mother or father she was going out, they would have asked her a million questions: Where are you going? Who are you going out with? What time will you be home?

But Margaret only opened the refrigerator and pulled out a lonely container of yogurt. Then she filled a kettle with water and put it on the stove. "How was school?" she asked.

"Okay. I had a meeting with my guidance counselor about college applications."

"What did she say?"

"Well, my grades are fine. But she thinks I need more extracurricular activities. The problem is, I can't think of anything I want to do. I mean, I can't sing or act, and I'm a total klutz when it comes to sports."

The kettle whistled, and Margaret turned off the burner. "Want some tea?"

"No, thanks."

Margaret put a teabag in her cup. "How about the school paper? Or the literary magazine?"

"I'm not into writing," Lindsay said. "I go

through incredible agony just to write a term paper."

"So you told me." Margaret sat down at the kitchen table. "I guess I forget that just because writing's my passion doesn't mean it's going to be yours."

No kidding, Lindsay thought. She couldn't think of a single interest she and her aunt had in common.

"Come join me for a while," Margaret said, pulling out a chair. "We haven't had a good talk in ages."

We've never had a good talk, Lindsay thought. But she sat down obediently. "So . . . uhh . . . what did you do today?"

"Just a boring interview with an idiot from the West Side who's running for City Council. He talked for four straight hours and didn't say one interesting thing. I'll be lucky if I can get two paragraphs out of it."

"Too bad," Lindsay said.

"Well, it's all in a day's work. I just wish I could get a more exciting assignment to work on."

"Have you ever thought about interviewing celebrities?" Lindsay asked. "You know, actors or rock stars?"

"I tried that once. They're worse than politicians. They've all got such massive egos." She reached down and pulled off her shoes. Lindsay eyed them. They were scuffed, and the heels were run-down. Her mother would never have gone out in shoes like that in a million years.

"My feet are killing me," Margaret said. "I

couldn't get a cab, so I walked back through the park."

"It must have been pretty," Lindsay said. "The leaves are all turning."

"I'm sure it was," Margaret said. "You know, I didn't even notice. I was too busy thinking about what I can do to make this interview halfway interesting."

She took a sip of her tea and her eyes glazed over. After three months, Lindsay recognized that look. Margaret was composing the article in her head.

Lindsay sighed. In all fairness, she'd probably lucked out when it came to Margaret. Her aunt could have been a busybody who watched Lindsay like a hawk and tried to run her life. Having Margaret around was more like having a roommate. Not a close friend, of course, but inoffensive.

She was kind and well-meaning, if a little scatterbrained. At least she paid the bills and gave Lindsay her weekly allowance. The two of them coexisted peacefully. So what if that was as far as it went? It wasn't such a bad life.

But it certainly wasn't the life she'd known before.

"Hey, Margaret," Lindsay said. "Would you mind if I had some friends over for dinner tomorrow night?"

"Of course not! I think that's a great idea. I could make some pasta and a salad. . . . I'm not the greatest cook in the world, but I could handle that."

"Okay. Thanks." Lindsay glanced around the kitchen. It had a microwave, a food processor, and every other culinary gadget imaginable. She thought regretfully of all the delicious gourmet dinners her mother had created there.

"Well, I'd better go get ready for my date," she said. Her aunt nodded. Her eyes had that faraway look again. Lindsay hoped Margaret was thinking about Saturday's dinner, but she didn't count on it. "See you," she said softly. Then she went to her bedroom.

It was a pretty room. The curtains and the bedspread were in the same delicate floral print—violets and tiny red roses. She and her mother had chosen it together. On the blond wood dresser there was a neat arrangement of perfume bottles, Lindsay's jewelry box, and a small gilt-framed photograph of her parents. Stuck in the edge of the mirror was a picture of Parker, looking gorgeous in his varsity letter jacket.

Lindsay pulled off her school uniform, wrapped herself in a terrycloth robe, and padded out to the bathroom. She ran water into the tub and sprinkled in some rose-scented bath beads. The warmth of the water and the sweet smell enveloped her as she eased herself in.

She let her thoughts drift to the problem of dressing for her date. What hadn't Parker seen? Two months . . . it was hard to believe they'd been dating that long. She still felt peculiar thinking of him as her boyfriend.

She'd known Parker for more than those two months, of course, or at least she'd known *of* him. Good-looking, athletic, popular—Parker Holland was a guy every girl at Benedict was aware of. But

Lindsay never dreamed Parker Holland was aware of her. Not until that day two months ago. . . .

It was summer, and Margaret had been living with her for a month. Lindsay still felt awkward around her aunt, so she spent as much time as she could away from home. She played tennis, went roller-skating, hung out in the local coffee shop, or sometimes just walked around window-shopping.

It was during one of those window-shopping excursions that she ran into Parker. She was standing in front of a boutique window, watching a live model pretend to be a mannequin. The model was posing in an outrageous dress—low-cut, skin-tight, and covered with bright red sequins.

"That dress would look better on you," came a voice from behind her.

Taken aback, Lindsay turned and confronted a handsome boy with wide-set gray eyes and sun-bleached hair. She recognized him instantly.

"It's not my style," was all she could manage to reply.

"No? It should be." His lazy smile was beguiling.

"You think so?" she asked.

"Definitely."

It wasn't much of a conversation, but that was how it started. He asked her out that very night, and they'd been going together ever since.

Parker was her first real boyfriend. She loved seeing heads turn when they walked down the school halls together, and she liked being known as Parker's girlfriend. They seemed to get along, too—or at least they seldom argued. Their conversations never got too intense. That was fine with

Lindsay. She wasn't sure she could handle anything more, not after what had happened. Even
though time had passed, she still felt numb, brit-
tle—as if she were made of glass. She didn't think
she could stand to get too close to anyone. It was
enough, just knowing there was someone there for
her.

The skin on Lindsay's fingers was beginning to
wrinkle, and the water was getting cold. She got
out of the tub, dried herself off, and put her robe
back on.

In her bedroom she studied the contents of her
closet. Finally she chose a dark green knit jumpsuit
that brought out her hazel eyes. She quickly fixed
her makeup and went out into the hall. Margaret's
door was slightly ajar. She thought of going in and
asking her aunt how she looked, then decided
against it.

The intercom in the alcove buzzed shrilly. Lindsay hurried down the hall and hit the speaker button. "Hello?"

"Hi, babe, it's me."

"I'll be right down." She stepped back into the
hall and opened the front door. "Margaret, I'm
leaving," she called out.

"Have a nice time," her aunt's voice drifted back.

Lindsay pulled the door shut behind her.

3

PARKER WAS WAITING FOR LINDSAY IN THE LOBBY. HE was wearing chinos, crisp-looking but not too pressed. His dark blue rugby shirt was immaculate but slightly rumpled, just enough to give it the right casual look. A green sweater hung down his back, the arms draped loosely across his chest.

He gave her an approving once-over. "You look great, Lin."

"Thanks. So do you."

He held the door open for her and they walked out of the building. "We're meeting Claire and Ron at Hunan Taste. Then, after we eat, we can go over to Woody's, that new place on Third Avenue."

Parker always planned their evenings together. Lindsay usually liked that. It made her feel cared for. But tonight she looked at him anxiously.

"Isn't Woody's a bar? Don't you have to be twenty-one to get in?"

"Nah. They let everyone in."

"We won't get into any trouble, will we?"

He tossed an arm loosely around her shoulder. "Don't worry about it, babe."

"Are you sure?"

Parker gave her a little squeeze. "Of course I'm sure. I'm not about to do anything that could get me into serious trouble. I have to keep on my dad's good side, remember? Because of that car he's giving me for my birthday." He kissed her on the cheek. "So don't worry about it, okay? Nothing's going to happen."

"Okay." Lindsay relaxed and let Parker guide her down the street.

Hunan Taste was noisy and cheerful. Parker spotted Claire and Ron in a booth across the room. "Hey, guys!" he called. There was a chorus of greetings as Lindsay and Parker slid into their seats.

Ron grinned at Lindsay. Lindsay smiled back, but not too warmly. She wasn't exactly crazy about Ron. She glanced nervously over at Claire Magnuson. She didn't know Claire well at all, although she'd certainly heard enough about her.

As usual, Claire looked fantastic. Somehow she'd managed to retain her summer tan, and it set off her subtly streaked tangle of golden hair. Her black, T-shirt-style dress looked simple, but Lindsay could see how well cut it was. Around Claire's neck was a slender gold chain, and she had on gold earrings shaped like tiny starfish.

"Great jumpsuit, Lindsay," Claire said.

"Oh, uh, thanks," Lindsay stammered. She was

afraid she'd sound really phony if she returned the compliment.

"I'm starving," Ron announced. "Let's order." He snapped his fingers at a passing waitress. Lindsay felt a little embarrassed, but no one else seemed to mind.

Ron tried to order a beer.

"Could I see your driver's license, please?" the waitress asked.

Ron slapped a hand to his head. "Gee, I forgot it."

"Right. I'm afraid I'm going to have to forget your beer, then." Her tone was light and friendly, but as she moved away Ron muttered an insult just loud enough for her to hear.

Claire eyed him. "Ron, you can live without a beer."

"Besides, we're going to Woody's afterward," Parker said. "You can drink as much as you want there."

Lindsay glanced at Claire to see her reaction. She didn't seem perturbed at all. But she must have noticed the apprehension on Lindsay's face.

"It's okay," Claire assured her. "Lots of Benedict kids hang out there. I wouldn't go anyplace where we'd get into trouble. My parents are incredibly strict. Are yours?"

Luckily the waitress appeared with their sodas. Lindsay took a long sip of hers before answering. Out of the corner of her eye she could see Parker staring off into the distance. He hated emotional scenes.

"My parents are dead, Claire."

Claire put a hand to her mouth. "Oh, Lindsay. I'm so sorry. Of course. I just forgot." Lindsay wasn't surprised. the accident had been on the national news; the fact that her parents were involved made the local stations. Everyone at Benedict had known that Lindsay Crawford's parents had died.

Despite her distress, Lindsay had to admire Claire's response. She had managed to admit she'd said the wrong thing without appearing embarrassed or awkward.

"I live with my aunt," Lindsay told Claire after a pause. "Actually my aunt lives with me. She moved in after my parents . . ."

Claire nodded sympathetically. "Do you like her?"

"She's okay."

The food appeared and they began to eat.

Claire delicately picked a sliver of water chestnut off her plate. "Well, I've got some interesting news, if you guys can keep a secret. You know my mother's on the board of directors at Benedict," Claire said in a low voice. "And one of the alums just gave the school an enormous donation."

"Whoopee," Ron said flatly. "What's that going to mean—more science labs? Really thrilling, Claire."

Claire smiled. "I haven't finished, Ron. You see, the donation has a string attached. According to the alum, the money can be used for one thing and one thing only." She paused dramatically.

"Hey, don't keep us in suspense," Parker drawled. "What's the money for?"

Claire's smile broadened. "A swimming pool! A great big one, enclosed in glass, that can be opened in warm weather!"

"Wow!" Ron bellowed.

"Pretty cool," Parker said.

"I'll say," Claire said. "How many other private schools have their own swimming pool? And according to the schedule, we'll have it by late spring. Just think. By next summer we'll be able to hang out around our own private pool."

"Wait a minute," Ron said. "Where are they going to build this pool?"

Parker reached for more rice. "Maybe they're going to tear down the school building," he said. He winked at Lindsay. "Then we can have all our classes underwater."

Claire and Lindsay exchanged looks. "Really cute, Parker," Claire told him. "But not exactly. You know the public playground right next to Benedict? Well, Benedict owns that land. They've just been letting the city use it, and that's where the pool's going to be."

"Hey, I like that idea," Ron said. "We can stare out the windows during class and check out the chicks at the pool."

"You know, Ron, you can be a real jerk sometimes," Claire said.

Ron didn't appear the least bit offended.

When they left the restaurant, Lindsay and Claire fell behind the two boys, who were busy discussing the school football team.

"Ron's so obnoxious sometimes," Claire remarked.

"Do you go out with him often?" Lindsay asked.

Claire shook her head. "No way. I've got a boyfriend, Craig. He's away at college though, and he couldn't come home this weekend. Ron called, and I didn't have anything else to do." She shrugged. "You know, Lindsay, you're lucky to have Parker right here in town."

"Yeah, I guess so."

"You *guess* so? C'mon, Lindsay. Parker Holland is a doll."

Lindsay watched Parker maneuver his way across Third Avenue. "Yes," she said. "He definitely is."

Claire was right about Woody's. It might have been a bar, but Lindsay spotted at least half a dozen Benedict people.

"Hey, there's Bobby Clark," Ron announced. "I heard he got suspended for a whole week for cutting classes. I want to ask him what happened."

"Yeah, me, too." Parker squeezed Lindsay's shoulder. "Be right back, babe."

Lindsay winced. She'd never been able to bring herself to tell him she hated it when he called her that. She glanced at Claire, who shook her head. "Men. Or should I say, boys. C'mon, let's sit down."

They found a little table in the corner. "Now," Claire said, leaning forward, "tell me all about your aunt."

Lindsay couldn't help feeling a little flattered. Cool, perfect, Claire Magnuson was actually interested in her?

"She's a writer. She writes articles for magazines

and newspapers. And she's written a couple of books about politics. . . ."

"How interesting!"

"Yeah, I know. She doesn't *act* very interesting, though." Lindsay broke off awkwardly.

"Why is that?" Claire asked.

"Well, she's totally into her work and that's all she really thinks about."

"Have you tried talking to her about that?" Claire asked.

"We don't have that kind of relationship. Actually, we don't have much of a relationship. We're both just sort of—there."

Parker, beer mug in hand, pulled a chair up to their table. "Who are you two talking about—me or Ron?"

"Isn't that typical of boys," Claire said, smiling at Lindsay. "They always think girls have nothing better to talk about than *them*."

"That's right." Lindsay turned to Parker. "For your information, I was telling Claire about my aunt."

"Geez, even *I'm* more interesting than she is. . . ."

"Don't you like Lindsay's aunt?" Claire asked.

Parker shrugged. "I don't really know her. I don't think I've ever said much more than hello and how are you to her."

"Well, I'm going to give you a chance to say more," Lindsay told him. "How about coming over for dinner tomorrow night?"

"Can't make it, babe. I should have told you sooner, but I'm going upstate tomorrow with my parents to visit my grandparents. Normally I'd try to get out of it, but like I told you, I've got to stay on my old man's good side."

"Can I come?" Claire asked.

Lindsay was taken aback. "You want to come over to my place for dinner Saturday night?"

"Sure I do. I think we'll have a terrific time. Especially with *no* guys."

Lindsay was amazed. If anyone else had invited herself over, she'd probably think they were being pushy. But Claire Magnuson—well, Lindsay figured, she knew she'd be welcome anywhere.

"I'd love you to come. Jennifer Gold's coming, too."

"Jennifer Gold," Claire repeated. "Oh, I know who she is." She smiled brightly. "Great. We'll have an all-girls night and gossip about every other girl at Benedict."

"Where's Ron?" Lindsay asked.

Claire wrinkled her tiny nose. "Don't trouble trouble till trouble troubles you."

Parker glanced over toward the other end of the bar, where Ron was still hanging out with the guys, tossing back a bottle of beer as if it were soda. "I can't believe that guy," Parker said. "He hasn't even got the decency to stay with his date."

Claire glanced at Lindsay. "Lucky for us." Both girls burst out laughing.

"Claire's great," Lindsay told Parker as he walked her home. "I really like her."

"Yeah, she's pretty cool."

"I think we're going to be friends." It was getting

cold outside, and Lindsay shivered. Parker pulled her closer to him. Something about the warm, protective feeling of his arm around her shoulder made her want to confide in him more than usual.

"I'd like to make some new friends," she began. "I mean, Jennifer's my best friend, and I guess I have a couple of other friends at school, but it would be nice to get to know some new people."

"Yeah."

"Parker . . ."

"What?"

"Do you ever feel lonely?"

"I guess. When I'm alone."

"I don't mean that kind of lonely. I mean, like, when you're in a room full of people, talking, and you still feel totally alone. Am I making sense?"

"No. What were you drinking tonight, anyway?"

"Soda." Lindsay frowned. "Never mind. I guess I'm just thinking out loud."

Parker didn't press her to explain what she'd said. Except for the fact that he sometimes got pretty heavy in the make-out department, Parker demanded so little of her.

Usually that was fine with Lindsay. For the past twelve months she hadn't felt much like giving a whole lot of herself. It was nice enough just to have a place to be, no questions asked. But that night, when Parker kissed her good-bye in the lobby of her building, Lindsay found herself wishing for more.

4

LINDSAY WAS STILL HALF-ASLEEP WHEN SHE HEARD the phone ringing the next morning. With a groan she rolled over and reached for it. The ringing stopped just as her hand touched the receiver.

She propped herself up on her elbows. The muffled sound of Margaret's voice in the hall floated through her closed bedroom door. As the low hum of Margaret's voice continued, Lindsay sank back down on her pillow.

She idly wondered whom Margaret was talking to. Some guy? Probably not. . . . Had Margaret ever been in love or had a boyfriend? Lindsay had no idea.

Rubbing her eyes, Lindsay got out of bed, pulled on her slippers, and padded out into the hall.

Margaret was hanging up the phone.

"Morning," Lindsay said.

"Good morning," Margaret said brightly. Then she looked back at the phone and frowned.

"Something wrong?" Lindsay asked.

"No. I'm just trying to make a decision. That was a newspaper photographer I know. The guy I interviewed yesterday is visiting a housing project in the South Bronx this afternoon. I'm wondering if I should go, too."

"What for?" Lindsay made a face. "The South Bronx is pretty scary." She'd never been there, but she'd seen it on the news. It was one of the worst neighborhoods in New York.

"Well, it *would* give me some perspective for my article. If I could add something about his experience in the Bronx, the article might have some pizzazz."

"You haven't forgotten about the dinner tonight, have you?" Lindsay asked uneasily.

"Of course not! Who's coming?"

"Just Jen, and a new friend, Claire Magnuson."

"Oh, I'm so glad. I've been wanting to meet your friends." Margaret glanced back at the phone. "I think I'd better go to this thing, though. Don't worry—I'll pick up stuff for dinner on the way back."

She disappeared into her room. Lindsay wandered into the kitchen and put the kettle on for coffee. While she waited for the water to boil, she peered out the window. The sky was thick with clouds. She turned back to the stove and turned the burner up higher. Making coffee was a skill Lindsay had had to learn since she moved in with Margaret. Lindsay's mother had been the sole captain of her kitchen, rarely allowing Lindsay to do much more than wash lettuce. Now she had to do everything on her own. Feeling a little sorry for

herself, Lindsay took a cereal box from the cup-
board and opened the refrigerator.

"Oh, no!" she groaned.

"What's the matter?" Margaret stood in the
doorway, dressed and ready to go.

"There's no milk!" Lindsay snapped.

"I know." Margaret looked at her. "I told you I
forgot to stop at the market yesterday." Unspoken
were the words, *you could always buy some things
yourself.*

She was right, of course. Margaret didn't even
drink milk. There was no reason why Lindsay
couldn't pick up items like that. But she'd never
had to before.

"I'll see you later," Margaret said, heading for
the door.

For once she almost sounded cross, and Lindsay
was sorry she had snapped at her. "Margaret, you'd
better take an umbrella. It looks like rain." It wasn't
exactly an apology, but as least she sounded car-
ing.

"You're right." Margaret took one from the stand
by the door. Then she smiled, waved, and was
gone.

Lindsay slowly ate her dry cereal and drank her
milk-less coffee. When she was finished, she went
back to her room and pulled on jeans and a T-shirt.
Then she went out to the living room.

She wondered how it would look to Claire.
Claire's home was probably much grander. They
probably had servants, too. It had been several
days since Rita, the cleaning woman, had been
there, and Lindsay noticed the mantel was a little

dusty. Margaret wasn't exactly a great house-keeper. Of course, that was another thing Lindsay could take care of herself.

Lindsay dusted, straightened lamp shades, and ran the vacuum cleaner over the rug. She was just finishing when the phone rang.

"Hello?"

"Hi, it's me."

"Hi, Jen. What's up?"

"I finally got *First Love* out of the video store. You want to watch it with me?"

"Sure. Your place or mine?"

"Our VCR's busted. I'll come down."

A few minutes later Jennifer was settling herself on the couch while Lindsay inserted the videocas-sette into the VCR.

"What time is Parker coming?"

"He can't make it," Lindsay replied. "He had to go upstate to his grandparents'. So I invited Claire Magnuson instead."

"You're kidding!"

Lindsay turned on the VCR, hit the play button, and joined Jennifer on the couch. "Claire's really okay. I thought she'd be snobby last night, but she was very friendly. I liked her."

"Yeah?"

"Look, just because she's gorgeous, popular, and fabulously rich doesn't mean she's a bad person."

"Okay, I'll give her a chance."

Lindsay grinned. "I'm sure she'll appreciate it."

They settled down to watch the movie.

It was a romance that had been a big hit the summer before. It was about two high-school misfits, a boy and a girl. They spent the first half of the movie pursuing other people before they realized they were meant for each other. They were finally about to kiss for the first time when Lindsay hit the pause button.

"Hey," yelled Jennifer. "What did you do that for?"

"Maybe I should call Claire and make sure she's coming." Lindsay bit her lip nervously. "I hope she's not expecting a feast or something. Margaret's only going to make pasta and a salad."

"Oh, dear," Jennifer said in mock dismay. "I'm sure Ms. Claire Magnuson dines on pheasant under glass every night."

"I'm serious, Jen. Margaret hasn't cooked at all since she's been here. She just picks up ready-made stuff at delis. I'm not sure if she even knows *how* to make pasta."

"You boil water and throw it in," Jennifer said. "Even *I* know that. Now stop worrying about impressing Claire."

"Who said I'm worrying about impressing Claire?" Lindsay shot back. But she had to admit Jennifer was right.

Jennifer hit the remote button, and the movie started up again. Lindsay forgot all about the dinner party. The romance in it was funny and touching. Lindsay felt a pang of longing as she watched the couple together. She recognized a depth to their feelings that she never felt with Parker. Perhaps it was something they would eventually grow into.

As the credits rolled over the screen, Jennifer sighed deeply. "That was wonderful," she said.

"Yeah," Lindsay murmured, glancing out the window. "It's starting to pour."

"Great. That's a good excuse to stay inside and watch TV," Jennifer said, reaching for the remote control.

The next time Lindsay looked at the clock on the mantel, she jumped up. "Oh, no! It's almost six! Claire'll be here in half an hour! Where's Margaret? She should be back by now."

"Where did she go today?"

"To the South Bronx. Something to do with this article she's writing. Jen, the South Bronx is a dangerous place. What if . . ."

"I'm sure she's okay," Jennifer said quickly.

Lindsay smiled weakly. "You're probably right. Maybe I should change my clothes."

"Should I change, too?" The way Jennifer asked made it clear she hoped the answer was no.

Lindsay looked her over. Jen's jeans were okay, but she was wearing an old T-shirt. Claire would probably think it was tacky. "You can borrow one of my shirts if you want."

Jennifer looked down. "Yeah, I guess this isn't trendy enough for Princess Di—I mean, Claire Magnuson."

"Jen!" Lindsay was cross. It was almost as if Jennifer wanted to wreck her chances to be friends with Claire.

"I'm just kidding!" Jennifer said. "What is it with you lately? I can't imagine you asking Claire to change clothes for *my* sake. But if you want me to change, I'll change."

Back in her room, Lindsay put on a bright green cropped sweater. Jennifer chose a long-sleeved, navy blue, striped T-shirt. They were both brushing their hair when the intercom buzzed.

"That must be Claire now," Lindsay said. "Where's Margaret?"

When she opened the door, Claire thrust a small white box toward her.

"I know you said not to bring anything last night. But I was passing Armand's Bakery on the way here, and I couldn't resist."

Lindsay peeked inside. A dozen tiny eclairs lay nestled in tissue paper. "Oh, Claire, you shouldn't have." She smiled awkwardly. "On the other hand, this may be all we have to eat. I don't know where my aunt is with the food." She led Claire into the living room.

"You know Jennifer Gold, right?"

"Of course. How are you?"

"Um, fine, how are you?" For all her wisecracks, Jennifer seemed a little awed at being in Claire Magnuson's presence.

"Can I get you a soda, Claire?" Lindsay asked. "And there's some chips and stuff."

"That'd be great."

Lindsay brought her a Coke. Claire took a sip and strolled around the living room. "This is lovely," she said. She paused before the portrait of the Crawford family. "And these were your parents," she said softly. She looked at it for a moment in respectful silence. "They must have been wonderful people."

"Yes," Lindsay said. "They were."

"Can I see the rest of the apartment?" Claire asked. Before Lindsay could reply, the apartment door flew open.

"Margaret! What happened?"

Margaret's suit was covered with red stains, her hair was tangled, and her face was filthy.

"It was wild!" Margaret exclaimed. "That idiot was talking to a group of housing project residents, telling them how lucky they are to have been given any government money." Her eyes sparkled. "And the project was horrible! People started throwing stuff at him—tomatoes, raw eggs, whatever they could get their hands on."

"It looks like you took some of that abuse, too," Jennifer commented.

Margaret looked down at her suit, as if seeing it for the first time. "Wow, you're right. I'm a total disaster. But it was worth it. I spent the whole afternoon talking to the people there. I got some fabulous material!"

Lindsay glanced at Claire. She was staring at Margaret with her mouth partly open. Lindsay couldn't blame her.

"Margaret," she said. "This is Claire Magnuson. Claire, this is—" she took a deep breath. "My aunt, Margaret Crawford."

"How do you do?" Claire said graciously. She seemed to have recovered from her initial shock. "Where did all this happen, Ms. Crawford?"

"In the South Bronx," Margaret said. "You know,

it's outrageous that people should have to live like that. I saw apartments with no plumbing, incredible fire hazards, and *rats*."

"Margaret, what about dinner?" Lindsay interrupted.

Margaret looked at her blankly. "Oh, no! Lindsay, I completely forgot!"

Lindsay waited for the floor to open up and swallow her.

But to her surprise, Claire didn't seem dismayed. "Don't worry. I've got a terrific idea. Why don't we just call Baldini's and have them deliver something? They have a marvelous pasta with duck and all kinds of great salads."

"That sounds wonderful," Margaret said gratefully. "Why don't you guys call, and I'll take a quick shower." She ran down the hall, and the girls went to the phone in the kitchen.

"Claire, I'm sorry about this," Lindsay began.

"Don't be silly. This will be fun." Claire picked up the phone and dialed. "I know this number by heart. We use Baldini's all the time. Any special requests?"

"You decide," Lindsay said. Claire briskly ordered several dishes. "It'll be fifteen minutes," she announced, hanging up the phone.

The girls returned to the living room.

"Have you guys met with the guidance counselor yet?" Claire asked them. All Benedict juniors had to schedule a meeting in the fall term.

"Mine's next week," Jennifer said.

"I had mine Friday," Lindsay reported. "She says

I need more extracurricular activities. Anyone got any brilliant ideas?"

"We could always use another body on a student council committee," Jennifer said.

Lindsay made a face. "But that would mean actual work. What I need is something that looks good on paper, but where you don't actually have to do anything."

Claire laughed. "Good luck!" She paused for a moment, as if she were thinking carefully. Then she asked Lindsay, "Have you ever considered applying to the Benedict League?"

"The Benedict League?" Lindsay repeated. "Isn't that like a sorority or something?"

"Well, you do have to be voted in, but I can't imagine that would be a problem," Claire said. "And it's really a service organization. We organized the landscaping of the little courtyard at school last year."

Lindsay had always thought of the Benedict League as being strictly social and exclusive. Maybe she'd been wrong.

"Would you like me to get you an application?" Claire continued. "You, too, Jennifer, if you'd like."

Jennifer didn't answer. She was standing by the bookcase, seemingly engrossed by the titles on the shelves.

"Sure," Lindsay said uncertainly.

Then Margaret reappeared. She still looked a little harried, but at least she was a lot neater.

"What a day." She sank into a chair.

"Lindsay tells me you're a writer," Claire said. "What do you write about?"

"All kinds of things," Margaret told her. "Whatever I can get, though I like writing about social
issues best." She sighed. "Looking at that housing
project today certainly gave me a lot of ideas."

"Do you enjoy working free-lance, or would you
rather have a regular job, like working at a newspaper?" Jennifer asked.

"I like the freedom free-lance work gives me,"
Margaret replied. "But sometimes I do miss the se-
curity of a regular job."

"Really?" Claire smiled. "Actually, my cousin is
the publisher of *New York Today*, and he's looking
for a society editor. You know, someone to cover
benefits, openings, that sort of thing."

"That sounds like fun." Lindsay looked at Margaret eagerly. "Wouldn't you rather hang out at
fancy parties than housing projects?"

Margaret laughed. "It certainly sounds less haz-
ardous, and it wouldn't wreck my clothes, but
somehow I don't think society writing is really my
thing. Thanks for the suggestion, Claire."

The intercom rang. "That must be the food,"
Lindsay said. She got up and buzzed the delivery
person into the building.

"My wallet's in the kitchen," Margaret called out.

A few seconds later there was a knock on the
door. Lindsay opened it. A tall guy in jeans stood
at the threshold, his face obscured by the huge bag
in his arms.

"Hi. Could you bring it in here?" Lindsay asked.

He followed her into the kitchen and set the bag
down on the table. Now that Lindsay could see his
face, he looked strangely familiar.

"Don't you go to Benedict?"

"Uh-huh," he replied gruffly. "That'll be forty-five dollars, please."

Just then Jennifer walked in. "Hi, David," she said in surprise. "You work for Baldini's?"

"Yeah."

"Lindsay, do you know David Jeffries?"

The boy looked at her curiously. His eyes were very blue.

"I think I've seen you in the halls," Lindsay said shyly.

"Yeah. I've seen you, too," he said curtly.

Lindsay might have seen him, but he was not someone she'd ever paid attention to. Now that she did, she saw that he was awfully good-looking. But there was something tough about him, too. He had a strong face, with high cheekbones, piercing eyes, and longish dark hair. Almost no Benedict guys wore their hair that long.

"David and I were in the same algebra class last year," Jennifer told Lindsay. She turned to the boy. "Remember Hitch the Witch?"

"How could I forget?" He grinned, and his whole face was transformed. He didn't seem nearly so threatening.

"I'll get the dishes," Claire announced, coming into the kitchen. "Which cabinet?" She walked past David as if he wasn't there.

Lindsay fumbled in Margaret's wallet. "Forty-five dollars, right?"

"Yeah," he said. The smile was gone, and his face was as expressionless as it had been when he'd first walked in.

Lindsay desperately tried to figure out the tip. It was one thing to tip a delivery person she'd never see again, but she felt odd and self-conscious tipping a classmate. "Here." She held out a handful of bills. David took the money and stuck it in his pocket without counting it. "Thanks," he said, not looking at her.

Lindsay followed him to the door. "Um, I guess I'll see you at school."

His face softened a little. "Yeah, maybe." And then he was gone.

Lindsay stood there for a moment, staring at the closed door. She could hear her heart beating in her chest.

"It's funny," Lindsay remarked casually as she came back into the kitchen. "I've never noticed that guy at school. Do you know him very well, Jen?"

"Just from that one class. He's in our year. I think he's big on the debate team."

"It's strange to see a Benedict student delivering groceries," Claire said, setting plates out on the table.

"Yeah, I felt sort of strange giving him a tip," Lindsay said. "But he's kind of cute, don't you think?"

Claire shrugged. "I don't know," she said. "But we're ready to eat."

They all sat down. The food was delicious, better than anything Margaret could have cooked. And thanks to Claire the conversation didn't go too badly either. She had a talent for asking questions that got people talking. Even

Jennifer loosened up and told them about some of the sillier meetings of the student council. Then Margaret described her odder writing assignments.

It almost reminded Lindsay of old times when her mother used to hang around with her and her friends, listening to their stories and telling some of her own. But thinking about it only brought back that dull ache that never seemed to go away entirely.

"This is fun, but I better get to bed," Margaret finally said with a yawn.

"I better get going, too," Claire agreed. "My boyfriend's calling tonight. I think he does that on Saturday nights just to make sure I'm not running around on him!"

"Maybe you should stay, and let him draw his own conclusions when he finds out you're not home," Lindsay said.

"It's a little soon in the relationship to really start trying to make him jealous. I'll save that for when he starts taking me for granted! Good night. And thanks, it was great."

When she was gone, Lindsay turned to Jennifer triumphantly. "See, I *told* you! She's nice, right?"

"She's okay."

"Oh, c'mon, Jen. She's friendly and charming, and she's not snobbish at all."

"Lin, are you seriously thinking about applying to the Benedict League?"

"Yeah, I might. It would look good on my college applications. Why don't you join, too?"

"I don't think I'd have much of a chance of get-

ting in—even if I wanted to. Which I definitely
don't."

"What are you talking about?"

"Do you know Connie Velez?"

The name sounded familiar. "Oh, yeah," Lindsay
said. "She was in my English class last spring. She
just came here from Mexico, right?"

"Right. Anyway, she saw the Benedict League
listed in the school directory as a service organization, so she applied. And they didn't let her in."

"Well, they can't let everyone in. They must
have had their reasons."

Jennifer grimaced. "Yeah, I'm sure they did. And
I have a pretty good feeling the reason was that
she's a scholarship student and speaks with an accent."

"You don't *know* that," Lindsay objected.
"Maybe they just didn't like her personality. Besides, why do you say *you* wouldn't get in? Just
because she didn't, doesn't mean you won't."

"I have a suspicion that if they don't take His-
panics, they don't take Jews either."

"*Jen!* You're being paranoid. Claire wouldn't be
president of any organization that discriminated
like that!"

"I'm not sure you know her as well as you think
you do, but if you want to apply, go ahead."

"I think I might."

"Why are you frowning? Are you angry?"

"No. I'm just debating whether or not I should
eat another eclair, Lindsay said," then Lindsay
shoved the pastry box Jennifer's direction.

"Well, one thing I do have to say about Claire. . . ."

Lindsay gave her a warning look.

"She's got great taste in pastries."

5

"I DON'T UNDERSTAND MARGARET," LINDSAY SAID
to Jennifer as they walked to school on Monday
morning. "She complains about how tough it is to
get assignments. So yesterday I asked her again if
she wouldn't want to at least *talk* to Claire's cousin
about doing some work for his magazine. And she
just said it didn't sound like her kind of thing."

"Well," Jennifer said, "you have to admit, the
subjects she writes about are more substantial than
a society column, Lindsay."

"I guess. But you'd think she'd at least consider
it. Just to try something different." They paused at
the playground next to Benedict.

"Those kids are so cute," Jennifer said. "Look at
those two in the sandbox." One was pouring sand
on another one's legs while the other happily
brushed it off.

"Yeah," Lindsay agreed. "I've got a seat by the
window in sociology. And sometimes when I'm

bored, I'll just stare out the window and watch them. I'm going to miss that."

"What do you mean?" Jennifer asked.

Lindsay bit her lip. Claire had said it was a secret. But it would probably be announced any day now. And she could never keep anything from Jennifer for long. "This land belongs to Benedict. And some rich person gave the school money to build a swimming pool here."

"A swimming pool! Fantastic! But where are they going to move the playground?"

"I don't know. I'm sure they'll find some place. Come on! We better get going, or we'll be late."

The girls joined the crowd of other identically dressed girls and boys in navy pants and white shirts pouring into Benedict Academy. "I have to put this student council notice on the bulletin board," Jennifer said. "Come with me. Please?" The two girls made their way through the crowd to the wall where announcements were posted.

Among the notices and messages, one caught Lindsay's eye. "Debate Club Meeting. Monday, 3:45, Room 210."

Jennifer noticed her studying it. "Are you interested in joining the debate team?"

"I have to join something, don't I? Even if I get into the Benedict League, I'll still need some more extracurricular activities."

Jennifer grinned at her. "Plus David Jeffries is in it."

"David Jeffries?"

"Don't give me that, Lindsay! I saw the way you

were looking at him, and since when have you been interested in debating?"

"Jen! In the first place, I *have* a boyfriend."

Jennifer was looking past her. "Speaking of whom . . ."

Lindsay turned. Parker was ambling toward them. "Hiya, babe. Or babes, plural."

Out of the corner of her eye, Lindsay could see Jennifer's face turn red.

"Sorry I didn't call last night. We got back pretty late."

"Did you have a good time at your grandparents'?" Lindsay asked.

"Yeah, sure, it was a thrill a minute. Listen, I have to stay after school for detention. Want to wait for me?"

"Oh, Parker. What did you get detention for this time?"

"Cut biology last week. No big deal."

Lindsay could see disapproval written all over Jennifer's face.

"Better be careful," Lindsay said mildly. "You don't want to get suspended like Bobby Clark."

"Yeah, don't worry. I'm not going to jeopardize my car. So, look, you want to wait for me?"

Lindsay looked at the notice on the bulletin board again. "Okay. Meet me in Room 210."

Parker saw the notice, too. "You joining the Debate Club? B-o-r-ing. At least it'll look good on your college applications, though."

"That's exactly why I'm doing it," Lindsay replied, avoiding Jennifer's gaze. She gave Parker a quick kiss on the cheek. "We better run, or I'll be in detention with you for being late. Bye."

Lindsay and Jennifer raced down the hall toward homeroom.

When they got to the door, Claire came hurrying toward them.

"Hey, Lindsay! I've got a Benedict League application for you." She looked over at Jennifer. "And you, too, if you want one."

"Thanks, Claire." Lindsay took the form from her and eyed Jennifer expectantly. Jennifer shook her head. "No, thanks, Claire. I'm so swamped with student council stuff that I couldn't possibly fit in anything else."

"Oh, too bad."

Was Lindsay imagining it, or did she see a wave of relief cross Claire's face? She quickly dismissed the idea. She was just letting Jennifer's accusations get to her.

She stuffed the application in her purse and made a mental note to fill it out that night.

Lindsay didn't see Claire again until she was coming out of her last class. She was standing in the hall with Elizabeth Dennis and Haley Gilbert— both members of the in crowd. Claire beckoned her over.

"Lindsay, you know Liz and Haley, don't you?" Lindsay nodded, feeling a little shy. Actually, she didn't know them at all except by reputation.

They both gave her friendly smiles. "You go with Parker Holland, right?" Liz asked. "His family and mine are old friends."

"He's a real sweetie," Haley added. "How long have you been dating him?"

"About two months," Lindsay replied.

"Wow!" Haley said. "How'd you guys hook up?"

Lindsay told them how she and Parker had met.

Liz laughed. "Typical Parker. He probably didn't even look at the dress in the window. He just wanted an excuse to talk to you."

Lindsay grinned. "It *was* a pretty awful dress." It dawned on her that both these girls were probably members of the Benedict League. Was this why Claire had introduced her to them?

The conversation moved on to a discussion of school and which teachers they liked and which teachers they despised. It was all very light and easy, but Lindsay couldn't shake the feeling that she was being evaluated.

As the little group broke up, Claire pulled her aside. "Can you get that application back to me by tomorrow?" she asked her.

Lindsay pushed aside a prickly thought that Claire seemed to take her desire to get into the Benedict League for granted. "Sure," she said. "Um, I'll find you before homeroom."

"Great!" Claire squeezed Lindsay's hand and disappeared down the hall.

Lindsay glanced at the clock on the wall. She was going to be late for the Debate Club. She ran down the hall and dashed up the stairs.

The meeting had already started when she walked in. There were only five people in the room. Lindsay was surprised to see that one of them was Ron James.

The other person she recognized was David Jeffries. His eyes flickered as she walked in. She walked over and sat down behind him.

"For those of you who are late, I'm Karen Johnson, president of the Debate Club," a girl standing at the front of the room announced. "We'll be having three practice debates this term. Then, in the spring, we'll pick the best team to compete in the district tournament." She sighed. "Of course, right now we only have enough people for two teams anyway. But hopefully we'll attract more members after the first debate." She picked up a stack of index cards and handed them to a kid sitting at the front. "Please write your name on one of these. Then I'll collect them and draw names for the pro and con sides."

David turned to hand Lindsay a card. She smiled at him and took it. "What are you doing here?" he asked without returning her smile.

"I just thought it might be interesting," Lindsay said coolly.

She wrote down her name and handed the card to David, who passed it to the front. Karen took the cards and placed them in a box. Then she reached in and drew names. "The following people will be on the pro team," she announced. "Ron James, David Jeffries, Lindsay Crawford. The rest of us will be on the con side."

David turned his chair to face Lindsay. "Looks like we'll be working together."

"Yeah," Lindsay said. "But, um, working together on what? I don't know what the subject is."

"That's right. You came in late. It's 'Resolved:

that capital punishment should be the mandatory sentence for first-degree murder.' "

Lindsay made a face. "How depressing."

David looked at her with slightly more interest. "No kidding. I hate taking the pro side for something I'm against."

"Ummm . . . yeah." That wasn't exactly what Lindsay had meant. She just found the whole subject unpleasant and didn't want to spend time dwelling on it.

Ron came ambling over and flopped down in a seat. "What are we supposed to do now?" he asked.

Lindsay was glad he asked.

"We get together and decide what our strategy is going to be," David explained. "Then we start researching."

Ron groaned. "That's what I was afraid of." He leaned forward. "Look, just between us, I'm only doing this to have something to put on my college applications."

Lindsay fought back a grin. They must have both gone to the same guidance counselor.

"Plus I'm no good at this research stuff," Ron went on. "So, why don't you guys figure it all out, and then just tell me what I have to do. Like, as little as possible, y'know? I've got to cruise. See ya around." Ron got up, grabbed his windbreaker, and left.

"I always end up with a jerk like that on my team," David said, fixing his eyes on Lindsay. He looked furious. She couldn't help noticing how blue his eyes were. *Ice blue*, she thought. "I hope you can do decent research at least," he said.

"No problem." At least Lindsay could say that

honestly. She'd always liked doing the background work for term papers much more than the actual writing.

David's expression thawed slightly. "Good. Why don't you give me your phone number? I'll call you, and we can set up a time to get together."

Lindsay ripped a page out of her notebook and jotted down her number. "I'm pretty new at this," she said as she passed the paper to him. "But I'd like to learn."

"I assume you wouldn't be here if you didn't."

"Are you this intense about *everything*?" Lindsay spoke without thinking. She felt her face go hot.

To her surprise, David smiled. But just as he was about to speak, Parker appeared in the doorway. "Hey, babe, let's blow this popcorn stand."

David got up. "I'll call you about the research," he said abruptly, and turned away.

"Bye," Lindsay whispered after him. Then she gathered her books and walked over to Parker.

"Who was that?" he asked as they headed down the hall.

"David Jeffries. We're on the same debate team."

"Oh." Parker looked bored. "I'm starving," he announced. "How about a hamburger?"

"We've got a bunch of leftovers from Baldini's at my place," Lindsay told him.

"Sounds good."

They left the building and headed down the avenue. "Parker, what do you think of capital punishment?"

"What?"

"You know, the death penalty for murderers. Do you think it's right?"

"Why? Are you thinking of killing someone?"

"No, I'm serious. That's the topic for the debate. We're supposed to argue in favor of capital punishment."

"I guess it's okay. I don't know. I never really thought about it. What did you do this weekend?"

Lindsay sighed. "Jen and Claire came over for dinner Saturday night. Claire gave me an application for the Benedict League," she added.

Parker actually looked impressed. "Hey, that's excellent. My older sister was in that when she was at Benedict."

"I don't know all that much about it."

"Oh, they do stuff for the school. You know, cake sales, junk like that. And they have this big benefit dance in the spring at the Tavern on the Green restaurant. It's supposed to be pretty cool, with a live band." He put his arm around her. "Let me know if you need a date, okay, babe?"

"You'll be the first to know." Lindsay glanced up at him. Parker *was* good-looking. Better looking even than David Jeffries and definitely a better dresser. He was a great athlete, too. *As Haley said, you're lucky to have him*, Lindsay told herself.

When they reached the apartment, Lindsay found Margaret stretched out on the couch, reading a magazine. "Hi. Are you feeling all right?" Usually at this time of day Margaret was out working.

"Oh, yes. I'm fine, Lindsay. Hi, Parker." Margaret held up the magazine. "I just got this. It has a story of mine in it."

Parker read the title. " 'The Insider.' Pretty cool. What's your story about?"

"Lewis Colby."

"Hey, I know him," Parker said. "He's a good friend of my dad's."

Margaret raised an eyebrow. "Really? I'm afraid he won't like this article much. Are you guys hungry? I was just about to go pull those leftovers out of the fridge." She got up and disappeared into the kitchen.

Parker picked up the magazine and flipped to Margaret's article. "I'm going to change out of my uniform," Lindsay said. "I'll be right back."

When she returned to the living room, Parker was scowling.

"What's the matter?"

Parker slammed down the magazine. "Boy, your aunt did a real number on Mr. Colby. She practically calls him a criminal!"

Margaret caught the last words as she walked in, carrying a tray piled high with food. "In a way, he is a criminal," she said, placing the tray on the table. "Not in the legal sense, maybe, but morally."

"What the hell does that mean?"

Lindsay looked at Parker in astonishment, but Margaret replied calmly. "He bought up all these middle-income, rent-stabilized apartment buildings in the city and found a loophole that allowed him to evict the tenants. A lot of people were thrown out on the streets."

"That's awful—" Lindsay began, but Parker interrupted.

"It was a business venture. Mr. Colby spent a fortune fixing up those buildings. He wouldn't have made a dime if he'd let those people stay."

"But what about ethics, Parker? Are you saying that a business venture doesn't have to be ethical as long as it's technically legal?"

"All I know is he's a friend of my father's. And he went to Benedict." Parker turned to Lindsay. "He's the one who's donating the money for the swimming pool."

"What swimming pool?" Margaret asked.

Lindsay explained. "It's supposed to be a secret, but we're getting a swimming pool at Benedict."

"Well, that's nice," Margaret said. "But I don't think it excuses what he did."

Parker glared at her. "I'm starving," Lindsay said desperately. "Let's eat."

"You guys go ahead," Margaret said. "I've got some calls to make."

"Your aunt doesn't know what she's talking about," Parker muttered when she'd left the room.

"Then it shouldn't bother you," Lindsay said. She felt a slight twinge of disloyalty for not defending her aunt, but she didn't want Parker to get angry and leave. "C'mon, have some of this pasta. It's really delicious."

Parker silently took a plate and started to eat.

After Parker left, Lindsay picked up her schoolbooks to take them to her room. A paper slipped out—

the Benedict League application. Pulling a pen from her purse, Lindsay took it to the dining-room table.

"Did Parker go home?" Margaret was standing in the doorway.

"Yeah." Lindsay was chewing on her pen and trying to figure out the proper answer to the question: Why do you think you would make a good member of the Benedict League?

"Listen, I'm sorry if I upset him. I guess I just get uptight when someone defends a person like that."

"It's no big deal." Lindsay was grateful that Margaret had disappeared until Parker left, but she didn't want to have a serious discussion with her aunt on the subject now either.

"What are you doing?" Margaret asked.

"Filling out an application for the Benedict League. It's a girls' service organization."

"That sounds interesting," Margaret said. "What do they want to know?"

"Mostly personal stuff. I guess it's just whether or not you fit in. It's pretty selective."

"You mean, it's exclusive? Like a sorority? I should think a service organization would take anyone willing to do service. . . ."

"I'm sure it's okay," Lindsay interrupted. "Claire's a member."

Margaret looked skeptical. Lindsay didn't want to talk about it. "Look," she said. "I'm sure my mother would have approved of it. She'd be proud of me for getting in. *If* I get in."

"I'm sure it's fine," Margaret said quickly. "Don't mind me. I'm just too curious for my own good."

"That's okay," Lindsay said. But it wasn't really.

6

Lindsay studied her face in the mirror. Concentrating hard, she carefully traced the outline of her eyelid with brown pencil then reached in her backpack for her lip gloss.

The restroom door swung open, and Jennifer came rushing in. "Are you okay?"

Lindsay turned to her. "Of course I'm okay. What makes you think I'm not?"

"I was down the hall, and I saw you come racing in here. I thought you were sick or something."

"No, I'm fine." But even as Lindsay spoke she could feel her pulse racing.

"So, what are you fixing yourself up for? And don't tell me you're meeting Parker, because I saw him leaving the building."

"I'm meeting David Jeffries at the library."

"All right!" Jennifer leaned against a sink ledge. "Come on, tell."

"There's nothing to tell, okay? David just has

some stuff to give me for the debate team. It's no big deal."

"Then why are you so jumpy?"

"I'm just being silly," Lindsay said. "I mean, I barely know him. And it's not like we have a date or anything like that. It's just that, well, every time I've seen him in the hall the past few days, I've gotten the funniest feeling."

"It seems pretty clear to me," Jennifer said. "David Jeffries is cute, he's smart, and he's definitely a cut above the average Benedict boy. I think you've got a crush on him."

"I don't know what I'm doing," Lindsay confessed. "I already *have* a great boyfriend. How can I have a crush on someone else? He's not even my type."

"I don't know about that," Jennifer replied. "Is Parker your type?"

Lindsay stared at her own reflection in the mirror. "Of course he is. I mean, isn't he everyone's type? All of a sudden every girl in school knows who I am, because of all the girls he could be dating, Parker picked me." She glanced over at Jennifer, who said nothing. "Listen, I better get going," Lindsay said, picking up her backpack.

"Let me know what happens," Jennifer called after her.

"Okay."

Lindsay hurried down the stairs to the school library. She peeked inside, but she didn't see David, so she positioned herself outside the door and tried to look relaxed. But when she spotted him coming toward her, her pulse quickened.

"Sorry I'm late," David said. "I asked the librarian to hold some books for us. Wait here. I'll go get them." He headed off toward the front desk.

Lindsay felt a tap on her shoulder. It was Claire. "Hi, Lindsay," Claire said. "Don't tell me you're meeting Parker *here*. I doubt he even knows where the library is!"

"Oh, no, I'm just . . . waiting for someone."

"Well, I was going to call you later, but I might as well ask you now. Can you come over to my place Saturday afternoon? Around two?"

"I think so," Lindsay said.

"Great." Claire smiled at her but didn't offer an explanation.

David returned, carrying a stack of books.

"This should get us started," he said. "We'll divide them up, and then we can compare notes."

"Okay." Lindsay could feel Claire observing them curiously. "Um, Claire, you know David Jeffries, right?"

"Oh, yes, you delivered the groceries from Baldini's the other night." Claire's tone was polite but cool.

David's expression was no warmer. "Yeah."

"We're working on a debate together," Lindsay added.

"That's nice," Claire said. "Well, see you later, Lindsay."

Lindsay noticed she didn't say good-bye to David. But he wasn't paying any attention. He was too busy sorting through the books. "Here, you take these," he said, handing three to Lindsay.

"Just go through the indexes, and see if there's anything that might support capital punishment."

"When do you want to meet?" Lindsay asked.

"We should get started this weekend. I'm working Saturday, though, and I have to spend Sunday with my family. How about Friday night?" The way he said it, it was almost a challenge.

Lindsay hesitated. Parker wouldn't like it. True, they hadn't made any particular plans for Friday, but they usually went out both weekend nights. On the other hand, just last weekend Parker had only told her on Friday that he was going to be away on Saturday. She shouldn't let him take her for granted either.

"Okay. Would you like to come to my place?"

David nodded. Then he looked at his watch. "I have to go pick up my sister." He started toward the door. Lindsay walked beside him.

"Where's your sister?" she asked.

"At the playground next door. A neighbor picks her up after kindergarten and brings her there. Usually my mother gets her, but she had to stay late at work."

"Oh. Where does your mother work?"

"Madison High. She's a librarian."

"Madison High? Isn't that dangerous?"

"Just because a high school is public doesn't mean it's dangerous," David said sharply.

"Oh, I didn't mean that," Lindsay said. "I just remember hearing something on the news last year about a drug bust there."

David gave a short laugh. "You think there aren't any drugs floating around Benedict?"

Lindsay shrugged.

They left the building together. David didn't invite Lindsay to come with him, but he didn't seem to mind her strolling beside him, either. When they got to the playground, he stopped and waved to a woman with a couple of children. She waved back and pointed him out to a little girl. The child came running.

Lindsay watched as David swooped her up, kissed her cheek, and set her back on the ground.

Lindsay crouched down next to the little girl. She had curly brown hair and blue eyes like David's. "Hi!" Lindsay said. "What's your name?"

"Sally. What's yours?"

"Lindsay."

The child cocked her head to one side and examined Lindsay's face. "You're pretty. Are you David's girlfriend?"

"C'mon, Sally." David took the child's hand. He turned to Lindsay. "I'll see you Friday night. Is seven okay?"

Lindsay nodded. After she told him her address, she watched them walk away. Sally was skipping to keep up with David's long stride. He had broad shoulders, Lindsay thought. Too bad he seemed to be carrying a big chip on one of them.

"Lin! Hey, space cadet!"

Lindsay turned. "Oh. Hi, Parker."

"I've been calling you."

"Oh, sorry. I didn't hear you. I was thinking about the debate team."

"What's the big deal? Ron says it's not much work."

"Not for him. He's getting the rest of the team to do his part."

Parker grinned. "Yeah, that's Ron all right."

Lindsay gathered her courage. "About the debate . . ." she began. "It's a lot of work. See?" She raised the books in her arms.

"You have to read all those?"

"I have to go through them by Friday. I'm meeting the other person on the team Friday night to go over the material."

"Friday night? You're not seriously going to work on a Friday night, are you?"

"I can't help it, Parker. It's the only time Da— the other person's free." She didn't have to let him know the other person was a guy.

"But I've made plans for us for Friday night. The new Starmaster movie is opening."

"Sorry," Lindsay said lightly. "You didn't say anything about it before."

"Well, I'm saying it now. Look, you can work on that debate stuff anytime."

Lindsay shook her head. "I'm sorry, Parker. It's all arranged. I can't get out of it."

Parker stopped walking. "Wait a minute, Lin. Here it is, Wednesday, and you're telling me we're not going out on Friday. Isn't that kind of short notice?"

"You told me last *Friday* that we weren't going out on Saturday!"

"That was different! I had to go to my grandparents. Which is slightly more important than working on a debate."

"It was important because you want a car! That's the only reason you went."

"Oh yeah? I guess the idea of riding in a brand-new Porsche with me doesn't mean anything to you?"

"Parker, this whole discussion is crazy. I have to work Friday night." She paused. "We can go out Saturday night."

"Oh, can we? What a privilege. Gee, thanks a lot, Lin."

Lindsay had never heard him sound so annoyed. "Parker, don't be mad at me," she said. "It's just this one Friday. Can't we go to the movie Saturday instead?"

"I don't know. I might have something more important to do."

"Like what?"

"I don't know," he repeated. "I'll let you know." He turned and crossed the street before Lindsay could reply.

Lindsay watched his retreating figure with apprehension. What had she done? *You've just canceled a date with the most popular boy in school, to spend the evening with someone who can barely tolerate you, that's what,* she thought.

It didn't make sense, but Lindsay didn't count on anything making sense anymore.

Lindsay took a sip of her diet soda and peered over the top of the can at David. She could barely see him behind the stack of books piled up on the dining-room table.

"Find anything?" she asked.

David closed the book he was reading. "No. Just a gruesome description of electric chairs and what they do to your body. I don't think that'll help our side much. What about you?"

"Here're some statistics on repeat offenders that might be useful." She passed the magazine to him.

As he read, Lindsay took the opportunity to study him more closely. She liked the way his thick black hair fell over his eyebrows. And there was something about his expression—determined, focused, intense—that she found intriguing. Even the way David dressed was different. Most Benedict boys wore cords or chinos when they weren't in school. But David wore beat-up jeans and a black T-shirt.

He closed the magazine and reached for his index card box. "Do you think the article will help?" Lindsay asked.

"Maybe." David started jotting some notes on a card. "But it would be a lot easier if we were on the other side. I'm finding much more information that supports abolishing capital punishment."

"It's pretty hard to argue in favor of something you're personally against," Lindsay said.

"Yeah. But it's exciting, too. It forces you to see another side of an issue. And it's great practice for someone who wants to be a lawyer."

"Are you planning to be a lawyer?"

"I'd like to be. If I can get enough scholarship money."

"You're lucky you know what you want to do already. I haven't the slightest idea yet."

"I can guess. You want to go to some fancy girls'

college, make your debut, meet some rich guy, have a couple of kids, and join a country club."

"*What?*"

"That's what all you Benedict girls want."

"How can you make a generalization like that about all girls?"

"I'm not talking about all girls. I'm just referring to Benedict girls. I can tell you about the typical Benedict boy, too. He wants to take over the family business, get a Porsche or a Mercedes-Benz or both, play a lot of golf, and have a summer house by the ocean."

"Wait a minute!" Lindsay exclaimed. "I'm not like that and neither is my friend Jennifer. You're obviously not, either. And we're all Benedict students."

"I'm a scholarship student," David replied. "Big difference. While you guys can just get by in your classes, I've got to study like crazy. . . ."

He sounded proud, and something else. Bitter, maybe? Lindsay was torn. On the one hand she wanted to defend her classmates. On the other hand maybe there was just a tiny element of truth in what David was saying. Still, she wasn't going to let him get away with putting everyone in his categories.

"I think you're being narrow-minded," she said. "Sure, there are some rich snobs at Benedict. But there are some really great kids, too. Just because some of them are well-off doesn't mean they're worthless human beings."

As she argued she felt a peculiar exhilaration. She'd never had an argument like this with a boy before. She was usually so cautious, so careful not to offend anyone or drive him away.

But David didn't look offended. On the contrary, Lindsay thought she saw a new glimmer of interest in his eyes.

"I didn't say you or the other people were worthless human beings," he countered. "But I'm sure you don't have to worry about things like scholarships. Your parents can probably buy you a place at any college you want."

"My parents are dead."

For a second David was speechless. Finally he said, "I'm sorry. I didn't know. Was it—I mean, did they die recently?"

"A year ago. In an accident, while they were traveling."

"Oh," he said. Then, a moment later, as if he remembered now: "Oh. Lindsay, I'm sorry. It must have been terrible for you."

Odd. That was the kind of thing most people said when she told them. But there was something about the expressive way David's eyes met hers that was actually comforting. Suddenly she had a feeling she could really tell him all about it, and he wouldn't be embarrassed or uncomfortable.

"It was . . ." she began. Then she caught herself. After all, she hardly knew him. She was probably just imagining that he could understand.

"You know, I've never been in a debate before," she said after a pause. "The idea of talking in front of a whole bunch of people makes me pretty nervous."

David smiled. "Don't worry about that. We never

get much of an audience anyway. Benedict students aren't exactly into issues."

"There you go again," Lindsay retorted. "Making generalizations."

"When was the last time you remember Benedict students getting actively involved in a cause?" David countered.

Lindsay was spared having to come up with an answer. The front door opened, and Margaret came in.

She looked surprised to find Lindsay at home. "Hi! What are you guys up to?"

"Working on a debate," Lindsay replied. "This is David Jeffries. David, this is my aunt, Margaret Crawford."

David immediately rose and shook Margaret's hand. "Pleased to meet you, Ms. Crawford."

"Please call me Margaret," she said. "I'm glad to meet you, too. What's the debate about?"

"Capital punishment," Lindsay said.

"Are you guys pro or con?"

"Pro, unfortunately," David replied.

Margaret made a face. "Too bad. I know what you're going through. Once I spent six months reporting on the campaign of a politician whose views were practically intolerable. Personally he was a creep, too, but I had to write about it objectively."

David nodded. "It's even harder to actually *promote* something you don't believe in."

"A real challenge," Margaret agreed.

Lindsay observed their conversation silently.

Once again she couldn't help comparing David with Parker. Parker was barely polite to her aunt.

"Anything exciting happen at school today?" Margaret asked.

"We had an assembly," Lindsay said. "Mr. Hanson, the principal, announced the donation of the swimming pool."

"Yeah. What do you think about that?" David asked.

"The swimming pool? It's fantastic! Imagine being able to take swimming in phys ed instead of volleyball! It's going to be really great for us."

"Great for us," David repeated. "Not so great for the kids who hang out in the playground."

"I don't understand," Margaret broke in. "What does the swimming pool have to do with the playground?"

"That's where they're building the swimming pool," Lindsay explained.

"But isn't that a public playground?" Margaret asked.

"Yes," David said. "But Benedict owns the land. They've let the city parks department use it for years. And now they're reclaiming it. A lot of people will miss that playground. Including my kid sister."

"And Benedict's just going to tear it down? That's terrible."

"Well, it's their land," Lindsay said mildly.

"That's true," Margaret said. "But it seems to me they should feel a certain responsibility to the community."

"Why?" Lindsay asked.

David's lip twitched. "Noblesse oblige."

Margaret grinned at him. Lindsay's eyes darted between them. "What does that mean?" she asked.

"Privilege entails responsibility," David replied. He glanced at his watch. "It's getting late. I think we've done enough for tonight." He started gathering his books.

"When do you want to meet again?" Lindsay asked.

"I don't know my work schedule for next week yet," he said. "I'll let you know as soon as I do."

"It was nice talking with you, David," Margaret called as Lindsay walked him to the door.

"Same here," he called back. "See you at school," he said to Lindsay.

"Yeah. See you."

Margaret was standing behind her in the doorway when Lindsay turned around. "He seems like a really interesting guy," Margaret said.

"He's okay."

Margaret just stood there, as if she were waiting for Lindsay to say more. Lindsay wanted to talk to someone about her confusion. But not Margaret. Lindsay had no reason to think Margaret would understand. Her mother would have understood perfectly. She would have appreciated how thrilling it was for Lindsay to find herself at the side of the most popular guy in school. And, Lindsay knew, thinking again of David's dark hair and his intense attitude, she would have understood exactly why Lindsay's heart raced in David Jeffries's presence. But it was useless to think about that.

"I'm really exhausted," Lindsay said to Margaret. "Good night."

"Good night," Margaret echoed, but her voice sounded almost wistful.

7

Lᴉɴᴅsᴀʏ ᴄʟᴜᴛᴄʜᴇᴅ ʜᴇʀ ᴜᴍʙʀᴇʟʟᴀ ᴛɪɢʜᴛʟʏ ᴀs sʜᴇ walked to Claire's apartment Saturday afternoon. It was only raining lightly, but she really didn't want to get wet. She had to look good, especially since this date with Claire could turn out to be her Benedict League interview.

She finally reached Claire's building. It was one she'd passed before and admired. A uniformed doorman stood under the awning.

"May I help you?" he asked politely.

"I'm here to see Claire Magnuson."

"Whom shall I say is calling?"

"Lindsay Crawford."

He went to a telephone behind a pillar, dialed a number, and spoke softly. When he returned he nodded and ushered Lindsay inside to the elevators. "Twelfth floor," he murmured as the doors began to close.

"What apartment number?" Lindsay asked, but

it was too late. The doors had shut, and the elevator was rising.

When they opened again she realized she didn't have to worry about knocking on the wrong door. There was only one.

A woman opened the door. From her black dress and white apron, Lindsay figured she must be a maid.

"Yes?"

"I'm Lindsay Crawford, a friend of Claire's."

"This way, please." The maid took her umbrella, and led her through a foyer lined with elaborately framed paintings.

"They're in the library." The maid tilted her head toward a series of intricately carved double doors.

"Hello?" Lindsay knocked lightly and at the same time turned the curved handle.

Claire wasn't alone. Five other girls were in the room with her. They all rose as she entered.

"Congratulations!" they chorused.

Lindsay was startled. Then Claire's tinkly laugh filled the room. "Don't look so frightened. You're a Bennie, Lindsay! You've been selected as a member of the Benedict League!"

"Oh!" Lindsay tried to recover her wits. "Thanks!"

"Sit down and have something to eat," Claire urged. Lindsay found herself on a small gilt chair with a plate of tiny sandwiches and cakes on her lap.

"You know everyone, don't you?" Claire asked.

Lindsay looked around. Liz Dennis was there,

and Haley Gilbert, and a couple of other girls she knew vaguely. "Is this the whole club?" she asked.

"No, we're just the selection committee," Liz told her. "You might like to know that you were unanimously approved."

Lindsay felt a wave of pleasure wash over her. She accepted a cup of tea from Haley. As she sipped it, she eyed the group. They were definitely all from the in crowd at Benedict.

"There are thirty members in all," Claire said. "But it's next to impossible to get them all together for meetings."

"Not that we have that many," a girl named Sheryl added, laughing.

"I feel funny asking this," Lindsay said, "but what exactly does the Benedict League do?"

"We ask each other that all the time," Liz said. "It's supposed to be a service organization, but it's actually more social."

"We do *some* service things," Claire said hastily. "Every Christmas we have a special tea at a nursing home. Plus we show prospective students around Benedict."

"And we usher the school orchestra performance," Eleanor Burton chimed in.

"But our *big* event is the benefit ball in the spring," Claire told her with a big smile.

"Who *does* the ball benefit, anyway?" Haley asked.

Claire gave her an exasperated look. "Benedict Academy, idiot! They use the money for school improvements. Painting and stuff like that." She turned to Lindsay. "I think you'll find the best thing about the Bennies isn't what we do, but what we are. We're like—a sisterhood, I think. Kind of one big family."

"Like a sorority?" Lindsay asked, vaguely remembering what Margaret had said.

"Mmm, in a way, only we don't have all those silly rituals and initiations. Mainly we're just there for each other. Like, if one Bennie runs for class office or something like that, she knows she's got all the others behind her. And if you've got a problem, there's always a Bennie to listen."

"Like just before you came." Haley said, "We were consoling Claire."

Lindsay turned to Claire. "What's wrong?"

"I broke up with Craig. He called me yesterday to tell me he can't come home again this weekend."

"And he expects her to just sit around and twiddle her thumbs till he gets around to making an appearance," Liz said.

"That's too bad," Lindsay said.

"Well, it was my own fault for thinking I could maintain a relationship with someone a hundred miles away. You're so lucky to have Parker."

Lindsay smiled weakly. "I don't know about that. Parker's not too happy with me right now."

"Why?" Liz asked.

Lindsay told them what had happened. "I've never seen Parker so angry. But he shouldn't assume I'm just waiting around for him to make plans for us."

"Are you going out with him tonight?" Claire asked.

"I don't know. He hasn't called. For all I know, we might be broken up, too."

"Maybe you should call him and apologize," Haley suggested.

"Apologize for what?"

"I don't know," Haley said. "It just seems like a shame to lose a guy like Parker over the debate team."

"Why did you agree to work on a Friday night anyway?" Eleanor asked.

Lindsay smiled hesitantly. Should she tell them? After all, they were supposed to be her friends now. "Well . . . it was with David Jeffries."

They all looked at her blankly.

"Claire, you know him," Lindsay said. "He was the guy I met at the library the other day."

"Oh. Right. That boy who delivers for Baldini's. I guess he's cute enough, in an offbeat kind of way. But do you really think he's your type?"

"I don't know, but he's interesting."

"Hey, you guys," Sheryl interrupted. "Does anyone know where the tea is on Tuesday?"

"It's at Linda's," Claire said. She turned to Lindsay. "That's Linda Ellison. You know her, don't you? She's a cheerleader. It's the mother-daughter tea, one of our annual events." And then she put a hand to her mouth. "Oh, Lindsay. I'm sorry."

"That's okay," Lindsay said automatically.

"Lindsay, why don't you bring your Aunt Margaret?" Claire suggested.

"Um, maybe," Lindsay said. She knew Claire was trying to be helpful, but she didn't want to commit herself.

There was an awkward silence. Claire broke it. "Would you believe I'm going out with Ron again tonight?"

Lindsay was happy for the change of subject. "Why? I thought you had such an awful time with him."

"I know," Claire said mournfully. "But I thought it would be better than staying home."

The conversation turned easily to a discussion of the boys at Benedict, and Lindsay was sorry when the group broke up.

"Thanks a lot, Claire," she said at the door. "I'm really happy to be a Bennie."

"We're glad to have you," Claire said warmly. "And don't worry about Parker. I'm sure you guys will get back together."

Outside the rain had stopped, and the sun was out. Lindsay felt elated. The Bennies didn't seem like snobs to her at all. They seemed genuinely to want Lindsay to belong to their group.

When Lindsay went into her apartment, Margaret was leafing through the mail in the hallway. "Anyone call me?" Lindsay asked.

Margaret shook her head. "Are you going out tonight?"

"Doesn't seem like it."

"I'm going to a play with some friends. If you'd like to join us, I'm sure we could get another ticket."

"That's okay," Lindsay said. Margaret looked a little disappointed. "Guess what?" Lindsay said, to make amends. "I got into the Benedict League!"

"That's nice! Did you find out more about what the group actually does?"

"Lots of service stuff for the school," Lindsay said vaguely. "Showing new kids around, that sort of thing. And they have a big benefit dance every year." She was about to tell Margaret about the mother-daughter tea on Tuesday. But for some reason she hesitated.

Margaret was frowning. Lindsay watched her apprehensively. What was wrong with the Benedict League now? But her aunt had something else on her mind.

"I was talking to someone I know in the city parks department today," she said. "Do you know that Benedict has absolutely no plans to relocate the park when they tear it up to build the swimming pool?"

"I guess they don't have any more land."

"People are going to be pretty upset when they hear about this."

"There are lots of other parks."

"Not close by. And not with swings and sandboxes and a big jungle gym."

Lindsay didn't know what to say. Then Margaret jumped up. "Oh, I almost forgot. I found something today I want to give you." She ran down the hall toward her bedroom. When she returned she was clutching a photograph.

"Here, Lindsay. Take a look at this."

It was an old black-and-white photograph of a boy who looked as if he was in his mid-teens. He was clutching the hand of a little girl who smiled shyly into the camera. For a second Lindsay was reminded of David with his young sister.

Then she peered more closely. "That's my father!"

Margaret nodded. "It was taken when I was about six. It's the only photo I have of your father and me together. I thought you might like to have it."

Lindsay swallowed. She didn't have any photos of her father when he was young. Only pictures that showed her parents together.

"Is something wrong?" Margaret asked. "Oh, Lindsay, I hope I didn't upset you."

Lindsay shook her head. How could she possibly tell her aunt it wasn't the sight of her father that bothered her? It was *Margaret*, standing in the photo next to him. The only person who belonged in pictures of her father were her mother or herself. She knew it was an irrational reaction, but she couldn't help it.

"Thanks," she said abruptly. "I'll go put it in my room."

She ran to her bedroom and closed the door behind her. She opened a dresser drawer and buried the photo under some clothes. Then she slumped down on her bed.

Less than an hour ago she'd been in such a good mood. And now. . . . That picture—it was like evidence, firmly establishing the connection between Lindsay and Margaret. But there *was* no connection, at least none that she could feel. She glanced at the photo on her desk, the one of her father with her mother.

Lindsay reached for the phone to call Jennifer.
But just as her hand touched the receiver, it rang.

"Hello?"

"Lindsay, hi, it's Claire. Did you know you left
your umbrella here?"

"Did I? Oh. Well, it's okay. I've got another."

"Lindsay, are you okay? You sound funny."

"Oh, I'm fine. Well, maybe a little down."

"Parker hasn't called?"

"No." She hadn't been thinking about Parker at
all.

"What are you doing tonight?"

"Nothing," Lindsay replied. There was a rap at
the door. "Hold on, Claire. Yes?"

Margaret opened the door. "I'm leaving to meet
my friends for dinner. Are you sure you don't want
to join us?"

"Yes. Thanks anyway."

"Okay. Well, I'll see you later."

"Who was that?" Claire asked.

"Margaret. She's going out."

"You know," Claire said, "I think we both need
something to cheer us up."

"Like what?"

"A party!"

"Who's having a party?" Lindsay asked.

"You are! Look, you've got the apartment to
yourself tonight, right?"

"Well, yeah. But it's already six o'clock. Who am
I going to call to come to a party?"

"I'll take care of it," Claire said. "It'll be a blast!"

"Gee, Claire, I don't know. It seems kind of spur-
of-the-moment." Lindsay had had parties before,

when her parents were alive, but they'd always been planned well in advance.

"Oh, c'mon, Lindsay," Claire said. "It'll do you good! And you'd be doing me a big favor, too. I really don't want to be alone with Ron tonight."

Maybe a party would do Lindsay good. Claire was probably right. And Lindsay definitely owed her a favor, after all Claire had done for her.

"You're right, Claire," she said. "I should have a party."

"I'll tell people to come over around eight," Claire said. "See you later!"

As soon as she hung up the phone, Lindsay dialed Jennifer's number. "Hi, it's me. Got any big plans for tonight?"

"Just pizza and a movie video. But I'm willing to listen to a better offer."

"How about a party?"

"Whose party?"

"Mine! Come on down."

Lindsay hung up and ran to the kitchen. Searching through the cabinets, she discovered a bag of stale potato chips and a couple of cans of ginger ale. Not exactly enough for a party. . . .

A few minutes later she heard Jennifer's knock on the door. "What's all this about a party?" she demanded as soon as Lindsay opened the door.

"It was Claire's idea. Margaret's out, and Claire's going to come over with a few kids."

"Oh." Jennifer didn't look too thrilled. "So you and Claire are great buddies now?"

"Jen, she's really nice. I got into the Benedict League, and they're all great. Honestly, you'll like them. Anyway you've just got to help me out with this party. There's nothing to eat in the house."

"Are you sure you should be having a party, then?"

"Please, Jen. I need you. Come on! It'll be fun!"

"Okay, okay. But only because you're my oldest friend."

"You're the best!" Lindsay grabbed a notepad and starting making a list. "We'll need sodas and chips, lots of chips."

"So now that you're a member, what's your first official Benedict League function?" Jennifer asked.

"They have a mother-daughter tea next week."

"Are you bringing Margaret?"

"No." Lindsay was surprised to hear herself say it. She hadn't realized she'd made that decision.

"Why not?"

Lindsay carefully folded her list and stuck it in her purse. "Because . . . she's not my mother. C'mon, we've got to get some food in this house before people start arriving."

8

Lindsay was frantically mixing onion dip in a bowl when the intercom buzzed. "People are coming! Jen, could you get that? I have to fix my hair."

Lindsay ran back to her bedroom, quickly brushed her hair, and put on some lipstick. When she came out to the living room, Liz and Haley were there, talking to Jennifer.

The intercom buzzed again, and Lindsay answered it. "It's Claire." Lindsay buzzed her in. She grabbed the dip from the kitchen and carried it into the living room.

"But I don't understand," Haley was saying. "Why wouldn't everybody want the swimming pool?"

"Because of the playground," Jennifer said, but Lindsay couldn't wait to hear more because the doorbell was ringing.

Claire, Ron, and four other boys from school stood at the door.

"I've invited a bunch of other people too," Claire

told Lindsay. "This is going to be the party of the year."

"Oh, no!" Lindsay gasped. "Claire, I'm not going to have enough food!"

"Don't worry," Claire said. "I'll take care of it. Let me just go make a call." The intercom buzzed again. Lindsay couldn't even hear who it was, but she went ahead and let them in anyway. Then she ran back to the kitchen to get more potato chips.

After a moment Claire was back. "Food's on its way," she announced.

"Thanks," Lindsay said gratefully as the doorbell rang again. "You know, this was a good idea. I'm feeling better already."

Soon the party was in full swing. Music was blaring from the stereo. The lights had been turned low, people were dancing, the table was laden with punch and potato chips, and new people kept arriving.

Lindsay took the now-empty punch bowl back to the kitchen for a refill. As she was mixing it up, Ron walked in.

"Let me give you a hand with that."

"Okay."

Pulling a small bottle out of a paper bag on the counter, Ron unscrewed the top and poured the contents into the punch bowl.

"Hey! What do you think you're doing?" Lindsay asked.

"You've been drinking this all night. I put a bottle in the first batch, too."

No wonder the party got so lively so fast! "Ron—" Lindsay began, but just then the intercom went off again. This time Lindsay didn't even bother to ask who it was. She just hit the entrance button and ran back to the living room.

Lindsay noticed uneasily that Liz was draining a glass of punch as if it was water. And off in the corner, Jennifer seemed to be getting into some kind of argument with two boys.

"Look, if people can't afford to go to Benedict, they've got no business using Benedict land," one boy was saying.

"That's an elitist attitude," Jennifer retorted.

"Whoa. Give me a break—"

Just then there was a loud knocking at the door. Lindsay ran to answer it.

"Parker!"

He stood there alone with a slightly sheepish grin on his face that only accentuated his blond good looks. "Heard there was a party. Am I invited?"

"Sure. Come on in."

"Sorry about losing my head the other day," he said. "I guess that was a stupid thing to fight about."

"That's okay," Lindsay murmured.

"Just don't do that to me again, okay?"

Lindsay smiled awkwardly. "Um, I have to get more chips. Why don't you go on into the living room? I'll be right there."

There were no more chips. Where was that food Claire had promised? "So, Lindsay," came Claire's voice behind her. "How do you like my little attempt at playing Cupid?"

"Did you call Parker?"

"Well . . ." Claire's lips curved in a smile. "I knew you wanted a chance to make up with him."

"I—thanks." There was another buzz from the intercom. Lindsay went and hit the button. Then she checked the action in the living room. Even though there wasn't enough food, her guests seemed to be enjoying themselves. Some were dancing, while others were gathered in small groups. A boy and a girl she barely knew were making out on the sofa.

"Hey, Lindsay," a voice called out gaily. Lindsay turned, and saw Liz dancing on top of the dining-room table. Liz was definitely having a good time.

In fact, the only person who didn't look happy was Jennifer. "I can't believe these guys," she said, coming over to Lindsay. "No one seems the least bit concerned about Benedict tearing down the playground."

"Jen, it's a party! People don't want to talk about serious things."

"But it's important!"

The doorbell rang and Lindsay ran to answer it. She pulled the door open impatiently. "Hello . . ." David stood there, holding two bags.

"David! What are you doing here?"

"Didn't you order from Baldini's?" he asked.

"*I* did." Lindsay turned and saw Claire behind her. "Put them in the kitchen, please."

Her haughty tone made Lindsay flinch. David walked wordlessly past her to the kitchen. Lindsay ran after him. Before she could say anything, Parker appeared.

"Great! Munchies!"

"Parker, this is David," Lindsay said. "We're working on the debate together."

Parker glanced up. "Oh. Sorry! I thought you were the delivery boy."

"I am," David replied stiffly.

Claire and Parker began pulling food out of the bags. Lindsay tried to smile naturally at David. "I'm having a little party," she stammered. "Sort of a last-minute thing. Um, could you stay for a while?"

"I'm working."

"Well, maybe you could come back later, after work?"

David just handed her the bill.

It read sixteen dollars and thirty cents. Lindsay fumbled in her purse and pulled out a twenty.

"You can keep the change," she said. The minute the words left her mouth, she knew it was the wrong thing to say.

"No, thanks." David reached in his pocket and counted out some change, then turned to leave.

Lindsay stared after him.

"Lindsay? What's wrong?" Claire asked.

"I think he's upset."

"Who? Parker?"

"No. David. He must have felt awful, coming here and delivering food to my party."

"Oh, Lindsay," Claire said. "That's his job!"

"I know," Lindsay said miserably. "But I kind of like him."

Claire shook her head. "Lindsay, I'm sure he's very nice. But let's face it. You can't compare a guy like him to Parker."

Jennifer came in. "Lin, things are getting a little weird in there," she warned.

Lindsay and Claire followed her out into the living room.

It was quite a scene. Several girls had joined Liz on the dining-room table, and it was shaking dangerously. The couple on the sofa were getting a lot more active, too. And over by the door, Ron, who seemed seriously drunk, was trying to pick a fight with another guy. "You jerk!" he cried. He threw out his arm as if to swing at his opponent and missed. Instead, he knocked over the vase with all the silk flowers in it. It shattered into hundreds of tiny pieces.

"What's going on?"

Lindsay whirled around. Margaret stood in the doorway, gazing at the scene. Lindsay heard a resounding whack and turned back around. The boy Ron was goading had responded. His aim was better, and Ron was now on the floor.

Liz jumped off the table. "I think I'm going to be sick," she announced.

Margaret hurried over to Liz and led her toward the bathroom. Meanwhile, Claire was struggling to get Ron on his feet. "Parker, come on. Give me a hand!" Together they dragged Ron toward the door. "I'll call you tomorrow," Parker yelled to Lindsay on his way out.

"I hope you don't get into too much trouble," Claire added in a whisper.

"C'mon, guys, party's over," Lindsay announced. Most of the people there took the not-so-subtle hint. A few just kept dancing. Jennifer turned off the stereo.

"I'm sorry. You'll have to leave," Lindsay said.

Margaret returned, minus Liz. "You want everyone out?" she asked. Lindsay nodded mutely.

Margaret briskly separated the couples. "Sorry, kids," she said crisply. "The party is over."

Finally they were all gone, except for Jennifer.

Margaret, Jennifer, and Lindsay surveyed the room. Glasses were everywhere, and punch had spilled out from a number of them. Potato-chip crumbs and scraps of cold cuts were ground into the carpet. Shards from the shattered vase littered the floor.

To Lindsay's amazement, Margaret didn't seem terribly upset. If anything, she looked somewhat amused. "This must have been some party," she commented.

"I'm sorry," Lindsay said.

Margaret brushed her apology aside. "It happens. Believe it or not, I was your age once."

Lindsay was floored. Her mother and father would have had a fit. She would have been grounded for life. But Margaret . . . Margaret was acting almost casual about it. Lindsay was glad she wasn't in trouble, but something didn't feel quite right. Margaret didn't seem even to care that Lindsay had thrown a party that had practically destroyed the apartment.

"Where's Liz?" Jennifer asked.

"Sleeping. What were you guys drinking, anyway?"

"Punch," Lindsay said. "With something alcoholic one of the boys put in it."

Margaret groaned. "That'll do it to you, all right."

"I guess we'd better start cleaning up," Lindsay said.

"Let's leave it till tomorrow," Margaret suggested.

"I guess I'll go home, then," Jennifer said. "I'll be back tomorrow to help."

Lindsay walked her to the door. Jennifer paused with her hand on the doorknob and lowered her voice to a whisper. "She's being great about this, Lindsay. My parents would murder me!"

"Yeah, see you tomorrow."

She walked slowly back to the living room where Margaret was sitting.

"I really am sorry," Lindsay said. "Some kids just came over and, well, I guess it got out of hand."

"I understand," Margaret said. She waved her hand as though she didn't need to hear an explanation. "You know, I once had a party when my parents were out of town. And it ended up even worse than this."

Lindsay smiled wearily. Margaret *was* being awfully good about this. Most people would have ended up in serious trouble. Lindsay knew she should be grateful.

"Uh, Margaret," Lindsay said, "the Benedict League is having a mother-daughter tea on Tuesday." It took a lot of effort, but she forced the next words out. "Do you want to come?"

9

Tuesday, at lunchtime, Lindsay came out of the cafeteria line with her tray and scanned the room for Jennifer. When she spotted her, she balanced the tray in one hand and waved frantically with the other.

Since the cleanup from the party Sunday morning, Jennifer had been busy with student council business, and they hadn't had a chance to talk. And now Lindsay really needed advice.

David hadn't called, not even to arrange debate research time. Lindsay had seen him twice in the halls at school. Both times he'd looked the other way.

Lindsay felt sick whenever she thought of David's expression Saturday night. The apartment had been full of people he considered rich snobs. And there he was, delivering food to them.

Lindsay smiled in relief as Jennifer hurried toward her. "Let's go sit in the corner," she said, but Jennifer shook her head.

"I can't now. I've got to get these passed out. Help me with them, will you?" She handed Lindsay a stack of papers and ran off.

Lindsay didn't even have time to object.

"Lindsay! Over here!"

Lindsay turned and saw Claire waving. Haley and Liz were sitting with her. Lindsay made her way over to their table and sat down.

"What are those?" Liz asked, looking at the papers clutched in Lindsay's hand.

"I don't know. Jennifer just gave them to me and told me to pass them out."

Claire took one and skimmed it. "Good grief. Listen to this, you guys." She read aloud: "Do we really need a swimming pool if it means destroying a playground? The playground is a popular community gathering place. Benedict Academy is part of the neighborhood. By tearing down the playground, Benedict is showing a lack of regard for the community of which it is a part. Think about it!"

"That's completely ridiculous!" Haley exclaimed. "We're paying the tuition. It's our land. Why shouldn't we be able to do whatever we want with it?"

"A lot of people use the playground," Lindsay said.

Claire looked at her. "But it's private land, *our* land. Let the city provide playgrounds for those people."

The way she said 'those people' made Lindsay cringe. She thought about David's little sister.

Liz glanced around the room. "There're a bunch

of kids passing these out. Claire, you don't think they'll get enough support to stop the swimming pool from being built, do you?"

"No way," Claire said confidently.

Haley leaned across the table toward Lindsay. "I still can't believe you didn't get into any trouble over that party Saturday night."

"Margaret hasn't said a word about it," Lindsay told her. "But then, she's been holed up in her room for the past couple of days, working on some big article."

Liz snorted. "*I* still can't believe I got away with staying out all night. My parents didn't even realize I'd been gone! I just told them they were sleeping when I got home and that I went out again early that morning. They didn't even notice I was wearing the same clothes I'd had on the night before!"

"You're lucky Margaret didn't ground you or anything," Claire said. "My mother would have wrung my little neck."

Lindsay shrugged. "Well, Margaret's not exactly the motherly type."

"Are you bringing her to the tea this afternoon?" Claire asked.

Lindsay nodded. "I feel I sort of owe it to her for not making a fuss about the party."

"She won't say anything about the party in front of my mother, will she?" Liz asked. "You know, about me getting sick and all?"

"Definitely not." Lindsay didn't know why she was so sure about that. But somehow she knew Margaret wasn't the type to tell. Margaret wasn't exactly the society type either, however. Since

Saturday, Lindsay had been asking herself two questions: How was Margaret going to react to the Benedict League mothers? And: What were *they* going to think of her? More than once Lindsay had regretted the burst of spontaneity that caused her to invite Margaret.

"Will you guys sign our petition?" Jennifer was back, standing next to Claire.

"Petition for what?" Haley asked.

"Some of us on the student council are calling for an all-school meeting to discuss the swimming pool and the playground."

"I don't understand," Claire said. "What is the point?"

"A lot of people are pretty unhappy about tearing down the playground. Maybe if we have a meeting of students and parents and people in the neighborhood, we can come up with some sort of solution." Jennifer put the sheet of paper on the table.

Claire glanced at it. "Jennifer, this is complete nonsense. If Benedict wants a swimming pool, it's nobody's business but the school's."

"But we're not saying 'no swimming pool.' We're saying 'let's discuss it.'"

"As far as I'm concerned, there's nothing to discuss," Claire replied.

"So you won't sign it?" Jennifer asked. Claire shook her head. Liz and Haley suddenly seemed engrossed in their food.

"Lindsay?"

Liz and Haley turned their heads now to stare at Lindsay. Claire was watching her, too. Lindsay remembered what Claire had told her about the Benedict League. *Bennies stick together.*

Her one signature wouldn't make a difference to the petition—but it would make a difference to the members of her new club. She could explain it to Jennifer later. Slowly, she shook her head. "Sorry, Jen."

Jennifer stared at Lindsay for a long moment before taking back her petition. Without another word she walked away.

Lindsay stood at her open locker after school and got out her coat. She glanced down the hall to see if Jennifer was at her locker.

In all the years they'd been friends, they'd had lots of little arguments. But she'd never seen Jennifer as angry as she had been in the cafeteria.

No Jennifer, but David was walking in her direction.

"David!"

He stopped, but he didn't smile or even say hello.

"I—I was wondering when we're going to meet. About the debate. It's next Monday. We need to practice, don't we?"

He nodded, still unsmiling. "I don't know my work schedule. I'll call you later." He turned to go.

"Wait," Lindsay said urgently. "Listen, David, about last Saturday . . ."

She didn't get any further. "Hiya, babe." Parker landed with a loud bang against the locker next to hers.

"Hi," she said hurriedly, and turned back to David. But he was walking away.

"What's the matter?" Parker asked. "You're looking freaked."

Lindsay closed her locker and started toward the door with him. "It's everything. Jennifer's mad at me because I wouldn't sign her petition about the swimming-pool meeting."

"Who cares? That petition is such bull. I don't know why those student council kids are making such a big deal out of it."

"But she's my best friend."

"Is that all that's bothering you? Look, you're in the Benedict League now. You've got plenty of friends."

Lindsay glanced at him curiously. Was he wondering about David and her? She doubted it. He wouldn't even consider David competition.

But maybe Lindsay wasn't being fair. Maybe Parker was truly concerned about her. Maybe she could actually talk to him about how she felt. "I've been thinking about Margaret," she said.

"What about her? She didn't give you any grief about that party, did she?"

"No. She was incredibly understanding. But it's weird. I keep thinking how my mother would have been so upset. I'm glad I didn't get in trouble, but Margaret certainly wasn't acting like a parent. Not that I think she could ever take my parents' place. . . ." Lindsay sighed. "I just feel so mixed-up." She looked up at Parker. "Does that make any sense?"

Parker was frowning. "Not really. I think it's great your aunt didn't get mad about the party. You're making a big fuss over nothing."

"It's not nothing!" Lindsay stopped. "Parker, this is my life! And I don't know what I'm doing, or what I want, or—or anything!"

"You're acting really weird, you know," he said. "Lighten up, can't you?"

"Is that all you can say?" Lindsay cried out. "I'm acting *weird*? Can't you even try to see it my way?"

Parker stepped back. Lindsay could see that he was afraid she was going to make a scene right there in front of the school. "Look," he muttered, "you better work out your problems, whatever they are. Because you're not a whole lot of fun to be around right now."

"Then maybe you shouldn't be around me right now," she replied. "Or ever."

"Yeah. Maybe you're right." Parker turned abruptly and strode off.

How stupid of her to think he might understand! How could he? How could anyone—Parker, Jennifer, or the Bennies—when she herself didn't even know what was wrong?

As Lindsay let herself into the apartment, she heard the printer running in Margaret's room. Lindsay walked down the hall and paused at the open door. Margaret, in blue jeans and a T-shirt, with her hair in a disheveled ponytail, was leaning over the machine, reading line by line as the paper emerged. "Margaret?" Lindsay said.

Margaret turned and grinned at her. "I finished my article!"

"Great." Lindsay smiled weakly.

"Don't worry, I'm not going to the tea like this,"

Margaret said. "I just need a few minutes to change."

Lindsay went down to her own room to change from her uniform into a skirt and sweater.

When she went out into the living room, Margaret was sitting at the dining-room table, addressing a large envelope. Next to it was a stack of papers—her article, Lindsay guessed.

At least Margaret's dress was okay—a plain beige knit with a tie sash. *Mom would have gotten much more dressed up*, Lindsay thought, *and probably even gone to the beauty parlor. But she's not your mother*, Lindsay reminded herself, *and she never will be. Don't worry, the Bennies know that.* Somehow Lindsay found no consolation in her thoughts.

Linda Ellison lived only a few blocks away, in a building almost as grand as Claire's. But the woman who answered the door definitely wasn't a maid.

"Hi, I'm Jane Ellison," she said.

"I'm Lindsay Crawford, and this is . . . Margaret Crawford. My aunt."

Mrs. Ellison ushered them into a huge living room. About forty Bennies and their mothers were gathered in little groups around small tables that held platters of sandwiches and tea cakes.

"Hi, Lindsay!" Claire introduced her mother to Lindsay and Margaret. Mrs. Magnuson eyed Margaret with interest. "I understand you're a writer."

"Yes, I am."

"Do you ever write about the arts? Ballet reviews, for example?"

Margaret shook her head. "No, my area is mainly politics, social issues, that sort of thing."

"That's a pity. There's a perfectly dreadful man writing the ballet reviews in the *Tribune*. I'd love to get someone more sympathetic in that position."

"My mother's on the board of the Metropolitan Ballet," Claire explained.

"That's a wonderful company," Margaret said. "I've been to several of their performances."

Margaret and Mrs. Magnuson began discussing ballet, and Claire pulled Lindsay aside.

"I just wanted to tell you how brave you were, standing up to Jennifer at lunch. I know she's a good friend of yours."

Lindsay smiled thinly.

"I knew we were right in selecting you for the Benedict League," Claire continued. "You knew it was important for us all to stick together, especially over something like this. . . ."

"Yeah." Lindsay's voice sounded bleak. Claire looked at her curiously. "Are you all right? Jennifer didn't get you too upset about that silly business, did she?"

Lindsay shook her head. "No, I'm sure we'll make up." She paused. She wanted so much to tell someone about David. But Claire definitely wasn't the right person. She clearly couldn't understand how Lindsay could have crush on David when she had a boyfriend like Parker Holland. Or was it ex-boyfriend?

"I've just got a little headache," Lindsay lied.

"Oh, too bad. Here, have something to eat." They started toward one of the little tables. Lindsay glanced back to see how Margaret was getting along. Another woman had joined her and Claire's mother. They seemed to be talking animatedly.

Claire left her at the table. Lindsay walked over to Haley, who was standing in the corner with a couple of girls she recognized but hadn't met.

"Hi, Lindsay." Haley turned to the others. "Lindsay goes with Parker Holland."

"I know," one girl said. "Lucky you! He's totally adorable." Lindsay smiled and changed the subject. Several other girls asked her about Parker, but she managed to avoid talking about their relationship. "Parker Holland's girlfriend" seemed to be the most important thing a lot of the Bennies knew about her. She wondered what those people would think when they found out that Lindsay and Parker had broken up.

They *had* broken up, after all. It wasn't just a little fight. For better or worse, it was over. Now she really was getting a headache.

Lindsay excused herself and wandered back toward Margaret. As she got closer, she heard Margaret say firmly, "But I think it's important for Benedict to have a good relationship with its neighborhood. Tearing down this playground certainly isn't going to help."

The two women with her exchanged glances. "But Benedict is a private school," one of them said sharply.

"I know this sounds corny," Margaret replied, "but no man is an island. Not even a rich man. Or a rich school, for that matter."

People were turning to listen.

Lindsay touched Margaret's elbow. "Margaret," she whispered, "I've got an awful headache. Do you mind if we go now?"

"Of course not," Margaret answered sympathetically. She turned to the women. "It was nice talking with you." They nodded stiffly.

Lindsay and Margaret walked home in silence. Out of the corner of her eye, Lindsay could see her aunt looking over at her with concern. But Lindsay kept her own eyes focused rigidly ahead.

As they neared their own building, she finally spoke.

"Did you have to bring *that* up?"

"What?"

"The damned playground!"

Margaret looked taken aback. "We were just having a discussion about the swimming pool. I think I made a valid argument."

"But it's none of your business," Lindsay exclaimed.

Margaret stopped short. "Of course it's my business. I'm a member of the community. And as the guardian of a Benedict student, I have a way to make my views count for something."

"Fine." Lindsay gritted her teeth and marched into the building. Jennifer was standing by the elevator.

Margaret came in behind her. "Hi, Jennifer."

"Hi."

Lindsay saw the petition in Jennifer's hand. "How's it going?" she asked.

"Okay," Jennifer said in a flat voice. "Margaret,

would you like to sign this?" She handed the petition to her.

Margaret quickly scanned it. "Absolutely." She reached in her purse and pulled out a pen. Holding the petition against the wall, she scrawled her name.

"Thanks," Jennifer said. The elevator doors opened, and they all got in.

"Good idea!" Margaret said to Jennifer. "An open meeting would really clear the air."

"That's what we think," Jennifer said. Lindsay stared up at the flashing floor numbers.

"See you later," Lindsay mumbled as the doors opened to her floor. She dashed to the apartment door ahead of her aunt, unlocked it, and went in.

Margaret's article was still sitting on the dining-room table. Lindsay glanced briefly at the title. She picked it up and began to read. The whole article was about Benedict's planned swimming pool and the playground. Her stomach started churning.

The envelope lay on the table, too. It was addressed to *Saturday Magazine*, one of the most popular weekly magazines in the city. Everyone read *Saturday*. Everyone would read this article, signed Margaret Crawford. And everyone would know it was by Lindsay's aunt.

"How do you like it?" Margaret's voice came softly behind her.

Lindsay whirled around. "How can you do this to me?"

Margaret looked startled. "I'm not doing anything to you. This is a community issue."

"Do you have any idea what this will do to my reputation?" Lindsay could hear her voice rising.

"I don't see how this affects your reputation. Maybe you should be thinking about how others are affected instead."

"Don't you understand?" Lindsay demanded. "I lost my whole family. For the past year, I've been all alone. And now, just when I'm starting to find a place where I fit in, you're trying to wreck it!"

Margaret turned pale. "But Lindsay, I'm your aunt. *We're* family."

"No, we're *not*. You don't know anything about me! And I wish you'd never come here!"

"Lindsay, please, just listen to me—"

Lindsay grabbed her purse and ran out of the apartment.

10

Lindsay stopped at the corner. her heart was beating so rapidly she felt as if she'd run a mile instead of one short block. Which way should she go? To the right? To the left? In the middle of the neighborhood where she'd lived all her life, she suddenly felt lost.

Imprinted on her mind was the image of Margaret's face—pained, disbelieving, stunned by Lindsay's words.

Why had Lindsay said that to her? For months now she'd cultivated a certain relationship with Margaret. They treated each other civilly, but they always kept a careful distance between them. It had made Lindsay's life at home bearable. Now she had shattered all that with just a few words.

Dimly Lindsay realized that she was cold, and it was getting dark outside. She had to go somewhere.

There was a phone booth on the corner. Lindsay fumbled in her purse and pulled out some change.

She dropped a quarter in the slot, lifted her finger to dial—then realized she didn't know whom to call.

Jennifer was still mad at her over the whole swimming pool/playground mess. Besides, she probably thought Margaret was wonderful now, since she'd signed her dumb petition.

Claire might sympathize with Lindsay's feelings about Margaret's article. But Lindsay wasn't sure Claire was ready to hear that the newest member of the Benedict League had practically run away from home.

When her thoughts turned to Parker, she knew she was getting desperate. If she called him, he would only think she was crazier than ever. Lindsay pressed the coin release to retrieve her quarter, then stepped out of the phone booth.

Slowly she turned the corner and walked up the avenue toward Benedict. There was a coffee shop there—Luigi's, where she and Parker used to go. It was a regular Benedict hangout, but it was after six now, so no one would be there. They would all be home with their families getting ready for dinner.

As Lindsay expected, Luigi's was practically empty. She settled herself in a booth in the back. A few seconds later a waitress appeared. "Hi. What can I get you?"

Lindsay looked up. She recognized the girl. "You go to Benedict," she said.

"Yes. I'm Connie Velez."

"I'm Lindsay Crawford." The girl nodded, still waiting.

"You work here?"

It was a dumb question, and Connie's smile broadened. "No, I just love to wear little aprons and hang around coffee shops."

Despite everything, Lindsay couldn't help laughing. "Sorry. Uh, just a cup of coffee, please."

"Okay." Connie jotted her order down and took off.

Lindsay gazed after her: *Connie Velez. She was the one who didn't get into the Benedict League.*

A moment later Connie returned with the coffee.

Lindsay took a sip and stared into space. She could make it last for a while, but not forever. She had no idea what she would do when it was gone.

"Lindsay?" The voice made her heart jump.

"David!"

"Hi. Can I sit down?"

"Sure." He slid into the seat opposite her. "What are you doing here?" she asked.

"I called you at home," he said. "To make a date for working on the debate. Your aunt told me what happened."

Lindsay groaned softly. "What did she tell you?"

"That you two had an argument. And you ran out."

Lindsay took another sip of her coffee. "She had no business telling you that."

"She was worried about you."

Lindsay looked up and met his eyes. "Well, she shouldn't bother. I suppose she told you what the argument was about."

"No, she didn't." He paused. "Want to talk about it?"

Lindsay hesitated. Then she shook her head. She knew where David stood. He'd take Margaret's side. It would be another reason for him to put her down and refuse to have anything to do with her. But then something else occurred to her. "Did you come here looking for me?" she asked.

He nodded.

"Why?"

"I guess I've always wanted to rescue a damsel in distress."

"Well, I guess you found one. How did you know where to find me?"

"I've seen your crowd hanging out here."

"My crowd?" Lindsay raised an eyebrow. "I wasn't aware that I *had* a crowd."

"You know what I mean. The Benedict elite."

Of course. She should have known he wouldn't change so quickly.

Connie reappeared at the table. "Hi, David!"

"Hi, Connie. How's it going?"

"Not bad. What can I get you?"

"Just a Coke, please."

Lindsay's gaze darted back and forth between them during this exchange. They sounded as though they were good friends. "You know her?"

"Sure. She goes with a buddy of mine, Pete Harris."

"Pete Harris? Does he go to Benedict?"

"No, he goes to Madison. Public school." He seemed to be watching closely for her reaction. She refused to give him one.

They sat in silence for a moment before he spoke again.

"You're in the Benedict League now."

"How did you know that?"

"Word gets around. I don't talk much, but I listen."

She gazed at him evenly. "And I suppose you think the Benedict League is a snobby, elitist, club?"

"I can't say I've ever given them much thought. I do know they didn't take Connie."

Lindsay stirred her coffee with a plastic stick. "I guess they had their reasons."

"Sure they did. She's on scholarship, and she waitresses in a coffee shop. Not to mention the fact that she's got the wrong accent."

Lindsay was about to protest when she realized she didn't have an argument. He was probably right. The Benedict League took girls like her. Girls who were socially correct. Girls with money. Girls who dated big men on campus like Parker.

But she had to say something in their defense. "I like belonging to a group. They're like a family."

David leaned toward her. "If they're your family, how come you're not with them right now? You look like you need some family around you."

She was getting angry all over again. She didn't need one more person telling her what was wrong with her. "I can see why you're into debating," she said coolly. "You're very good at it."

"Thank you."

"But you're not always right, you know. Some of the girls are okay. You've just got them all labeled. Maybe you're the one who's a snob."

"Me, a snob?"

"Well, the way you were acting Saturday night—" she stopped abruptly as his face darkened.

"Oh, yeah, Saturday night. You were about to say something to me about that this afternoon. Until your boyfriend came along."

"He's not my boyfriend. Not anymore. We broke up."

"Go on," he said.

"You weren't very friendly Saturday night."

"Well, how did you expect me to act? If you want me to be honest, I thought it was pretty obnoxious for you to call and have me come deliver food to your rich friends."

"You know, you've got a pretty big chip on your shoulder! You think just because you're on scholarship, everyone looks down on you." He opened his mouth, but she wouldn't let him speak. "First of all, it wasn't me who called. Claire Magnuson did. And in case you forgot, I asked you to come back and join us after work. And they weren't all snobs anyway. I was there. And so was Jennifer Gold."

"Okay, maybe I jump to conclusions. I'm sorry."

"You're forgiven."

"Jennifer Gold," David repeated. "She's doing a lot of good work to save the playground. She's a friend of yours, right?"

"She's my best friend. Well, she *was*."

"Was?"

"We had a little fight."

"Sounds like you're fighting with everybody these days."

"Yeah, it looks that way, doesn't it? Jennifer,

Margaret, Parker. . . . I don't mind so much about Parker, though."

"I thought he was your boyfriend."

"He's okay, I guess. But we never really had much going for us. I don't know. He was just there when I needed someone to be with."

David's voice was gentle. "It must have been rough for you. When your parents died."

Lindsay nodded. She didn't trust herself to speak. Then, to her horror, she felt tears forming in her eyes. She turned her face to the wall.

She felt David's hand on hers. When she thought she had the tears under control, she looked back.

"Your aunt cares about you a lot. I could tell when I talked to her."

Lindsay didn't reply.

"She's your family now—" David started to say, but Lindsay stopped him.

"No, she's not. She lives with me. That's all. It's not the same as—as having parents."

"Is that what you want her to be? A parent?"

"No!" Lindsay took a last sip of her coffee. "I don't know what I want her to be. That doesn't make much sense, does it?"

"Sure it does," David said. "I think it all comes down to the fact that you two haven't figured out what your relationship is."

"David, I don't want to talk about it, okay?"

"You don't have to. Besides, it's not me you should be talking about that with. It's her."

Lindsay didn't have an answer for that. She wanted to change the subject. "What about the debate? When are we going to work on it?"

"Well, we could work Friday night again."

"Okay. Um, could we go someplace besides my apartment?"

"You want to come to my place? That is, if you don't mind coming to the wild West Side." He grinned.

Lindsay grinned back. "I'll bring my passport."

"You guys want the check now?" Connie was standing at the table.

"Thanks," David said, taking it from her and counting out a couple of dollars.

Connie looked at the two of them with interest. "Listen," she said suddenly, "Pete and I are going to the movies Friday night. You want to join us?"

"We're working on a debate," David said. "But if we finish early . . ." he looked at Lindsay. "Want to?"

"Yes," she said. "I'd like that."

Connie beamed. "Great! I'll let you know what time."

She left the table. "I guess I should go back . . . home," Lindsay said. The word stuck in her throat. She dreaded facing Margaret, but she had to do it sooner or later.

David got up. "C'mon. I'll walk you."

They were quiet on the short walk back. But it was a comfortable silence. They'd said a lot already. When they reached the building, they both just stood there, looking at each other. Then David leaned over and kissed her lightly on the lips. "Good luck," he whispered.

Margaret was in the living room, reading. She looked up as Lindsay came in. Even in the dim light Lindsay could see the worry on her face. But all she said was, "I'm glad you're back."

"Look, I'm sorry about what I said before. I've just been kind of tense lately," Lindsay said lamely.

"I should have told you about the article."

"No, you were right. It's none of my business what you do."

"That's not true." The silence that followed was full of unspoken words, but all Lindsay could manage to say was, "I'm tired. I think I'll go to bed."

She didn't wait to hear Margaret's response.

11

FOR THE REST OF THE WEEK LINDSAY BURIED HERSELF in debate research. At least it gave her a perfectly legitimate excuse to avoid everyone, which was exactly what she wanted. Friday morning Claire finally grabbed her in the hall.

"Where have you been?"

"I've been swamped," Lindsay replied. "Debate research, you know?"

"Well, come sit with us at lunch today." It sounded more like an order than an invitation. Lindsay nodded. The Bennies were going to find out about her breakup with Parker sooner or later. She might as well get it over with.

When she joined Haley and Liz at lunch, however, she had a feeling from the expressions on their faces that they already knew.

"Okay, what's going on?" Claire demanded.

Lindsay feigned innocence. "What are you talking about?"

"We just heard that Parker asked Linda Ellison out Friday night," Haley said.

"Well, he has to go out with somebody. We broke up."

"Oh, no! What happened?" Claire cried.

"It's okay," Lindsay assured her. "I'm not devastated or anything."

Liz eyed her suspiciously. "You're taking this awfully well. I'd be hysterical."

"She's just putting up a brave front," Claire announced. "I was the same way when Craig and I broke up. And look what happened."

"What?" Lindsay asked.

"We're back together again! He's coming to see me this weekend. You'll get back with Parker, too."

No, I won't, Lindsay thought.

"In the meantime," Claire went on, "Craig's bringing a friend to New York with him. I need to fix him up. You want to go out with us tonight, Lindsay?"

"Tonight? I'm sorry. I can't. I'm going to be working on the debate with David. By the way, it's Monday after school, in room 356. Spread the word, okay?" She pictured David's face when thirty Benedict League girls appeared to hear the debate team. He'd insisted they'd never get an audience because Benedict kids didn't care about issues. Now he'd see that Bennies did stick together.

"I can't believe you're working on a Friday night again!" Claire exclaimed. "What about a social life, Lindsay?"

"Well, we might go to the movies after we finish the debate stuff."

"Who *is* this David person anyway?" Haley asked.

"David Jeffries."

"David Jeffries," Haley repeated. "I've never heard of him."

Claire was looking at Lindsay strangely. "You're not seriously thinking about getting involved with him, are you?"

Lindsay blushed. "I don't know. Why?"

Claire looked uncomfortable. "Well . . ." For the first time since Lindsay had known her, she actually seemed to be having difficulty deciding what to say.

"I'm sure he's very nice and all that. But he isn't really your type, is he?"

"What do you mean?" Lindsay grinned. "I'm not even sure I know what my type is, so how could you?"

"Lindsay, you know what I mean."

Something about her tone made Lindsay stop smiling. "No, I don't."

But the others did. "Oh, I get it," Haley said. "Is he NOKD?"

Claire gave her an almost imperceptible nod.

"What does NOKD mean?" Lindsay asked.

Claire smiled gently. " 'Not Our Kind, Dear.' Okay, I know it sounds snotty. But face it, Lindsay. Can you picture taking a guy like David Jeffries to the Benedict League benefit ball?"

Lindsay tried to picture it. It was impossible. David would hate an affair like that.

"Of course, you can date anyone you want,"

Claire added quickly. "But you don't want to get serious about a guy like that."

A guy like that? Surely Claire hadn't meant that to sound the way it did.

"Look!" Liz said suddenly. Everyone followed her eyes. Someone from the student council was tacking a big poster on the cafeteria wall. "Open Meeting," Lindsay read softly. "For all concerned with Benedict Academy and the community."

"Oh, for crying out loud," Haley groaned. "It's that playground stuff again."

"Tuesday, eight P.M.," Claire read. "I think we should all go."

"Why?" Liz asked, making a face. "Who wants to listen to a lot of people arguing?"

"We have to show support for the school," Claire insisted. "That's what the Benedict League is all about."

"But no one can really stop us from building a swimming pool," Haley said.

Lindsay poked at her food. She couldn't help thinking about Margaret's article. Should she mention it now? Or was it better to act just as shocked as Claire and the other Bennies would be when the article came out?

"It's the principle of the thing," Claire continued. "We have to show those people that they can't tell Benedict Academy what to do. I want all the Bennies there, sitting together. In fact, I think we should have a meeting first, right after school on Tuesday, and come up with some sort of position statement to present."

"That's a good idea," Liz said. "So long as I don't have to read it!"

"Don't worry. *I'll* do it," Claire said. "Lindsay, do you think your aunt's going to come to the meeting?"

"Probably," Lindsay said. "I'm sure she'll hear about it."

"And I bet she'll say something, too," Haley noted. "Like she did at the tea."

Lindsay nodded slowly.

"How awful for you," Claire said sympathetically. "Your aunt on one side, and you on the other."

Lindsay was silent for a moment. "It won't be so awful," she said finally. She got up. "I have to go to the library and do a little more work. I'll see you guys later. And don't forget about the debate Monday, okay?"

She hurried down the hall to the school library. By the library door she ran into Jennifer. She was putting up another sign about the meeting.

"Hi, Jen."

Jennifer punched the last tack in the wall and turned. "Hi, Lin." She cocked her head toward the sign. "You gonna come?"

Lindsay nodded. "Jen . . . are you still mad because I wouldn't sign your petition?"

"No. I mean, I was at first. But you have to do what you think is right." She paused. "I just hope you're doing what *you* think, and not what someone else is telling you to think," she added hesitantly.

"Yeah." Lindsay looked away.

"How's Margaret?" Jennifer asked.

Lindsay sighed. Another topic she didn't want to discuss.

"Fine," she said. Then she added, "I've got a date with David Jeffries tonight. Well, sort of a date. We're working on the debate, but we might go to a movie afterward."

"Lin! That's fantastic!" Jennifer exclaimed. "But what happened with Parker?"

"We broke up."

"I always said you could do better!"

"I hope you're right."

Jennifer nodded toward a stack of posters. "I have to go put the rest of these up."

"Okay. Listen . . . maybe we could get together this weekend."

"I'm really sorry. I can't. We're driving to Connecticut Saturday morning. My father's got his annual urge to see the autumn leaves. We won't be back till late Sunday."

"Oh." Lindsay tried to hide her disappointment.

"Look," Jennifer said. "I'm coming to your debate on Monday. Let's go out when it's over, okay? If you guys win, we can have a celebration. And if you lose, I'll console you."

"Okay," Lindsay agreed. But as Jennifer gathered her posters, it occurred to Lindsay that if all the Bennies came, they'd probably want to go out with her after, too. And if her team won, David would want to celebrate. Somehow she couldn't imagine all of them heading for Luigi's together.

* * *

"Going out?" Margaret stood in Lindsay's bedroom doorway.

"Yes. I'm meeting David."

"That's great!"

"We're just working on the debate," Lindsay said.

"Well, you look very nice."

"Do I?" Despite her resolve to keep as much distance as possible between herself and Margaret, Lindsay couldn't stop herself. "Really? I don't look too dressed up? I mean, I want to look good. But I don't want to look like I worked too hard at it."

Margaret laughed. "I know exactly what you mean. You never want a guy to know you spent hours getting ready for him."

"Right! Because then he'll think—" Lindsay caught herself. "That you care." It was strange. This was the kind of conversation she never had with Margaret. She hesitated, then she picked up her jacket and her backpack stuffed with books about crime and punishment. "Well, I'll see you."

"Have a good time."

Outside the building, Lindsay hailed a cab.

It took the driver only a few minutes to cross Central Park.

David lived on a nice block with large brick apartment buildings and plenty of trees. There was no doorman outside his building—just an intercom. Lindsay searched the list of tenants for Jeffries before pressing the buzzer.

A woman's voice responded. "Yes?"

Lindsay moved closer to the speaker. "It's Lindsay Crawford, David's friend."

"Come up. It's the seventh floor."

A plump, pretty woman opened the door. "Hi, Lindsay," she said with a warm smile. "I'm David's mother. Come on in."

Lindsay followed Mrs. Jeffries through the foyer to the dining room. "You're just in time for dessert. Or maybe you'd like some chicken. There's plenty left."

"Mom!" David jumped up from the table. "We've got work to do."

"Maybe Lindsay's hungry," Mrs. Jeffries objected. "Are you hungry, Lindsay?"

"A little," she admitted.

No sooner had the words left her mouth than a platter of chicken appeared on the table along with a bowl of string beans. David introduced her to the others at the table.

"This is my dad, and that's my brother, Chuck. And you've already met Sally."

Chuck, who looked around college age, smiled at her. Sally giggled.

"What are you kids doing tonight?" Mr. Jeffries asked.

"We're working on a debate for school," David told him.

Mr. Jeffries's eyebrows shot up. "Working! On a Friday night?" he asked in exaggerated astonishment. "What's the matter with you kids? Weekend nights are for good times."

"Well, we might go to a movie later, if we finish early enough," David replied.

"Lindsay, are you a workaholic like my son?" Mrs. Jeffries asked.

"Not really."

"Good!" Mr. Jeffries exclaimed. "David could use more friends who know how to have a little fun once in a while."

"Dad!" David reddened.

Chuck got up from the table. "Speaking of fun, I've got a date. Nice meeting you, Lindsay."

"Have a good time," Mrs. Jeffries called out. She turned to Lindsay. "How's that chicken?"

Lindsay was embarrassed to see that she'd consumed every bite. "It was delicious. Thank you."

"What's the debate about?" Mrs. Jeffries asked. Before either David or Lindsay could answer, Sally asked, "What's a debate?"

Mr. Jeffries wiggled his eyebrows at her. "It's what you use to catch de fish."

"Dad," David groaned. Lindsay giggled. It was the same kind of awful joke her father used to make.

"Hey, she appreciates my sophisticated sense of humor!" Mr. Jeffries exclaimed. "David, I like this girl."

"She's David's girlfriend," Sally piped up.

Now David's face was flaming. It was all Lindsay could do to keep from bursting out laughing.

"She's a friend who happens to be a girl," David's mother said briskly. "More chicken, Lindsay? A piece of pie?"

"No, thank you," Lindsay said.

"Then you just sit there and let me clear the table. Now everyone out of here so David and Lindsay can work."

"Yes, ma'am," Mr. Jeffries said, getting up immediately. "See you later, Lindsay."

Sally skipped over to her. "You know what?" she said confidingly. "You don't seem like a snob to *me*." Then she ran out of the room.

Lindsay looked at David. What had he told his family? That she was some rich snob? David looked as if he wished he could vanish into thin air.

"Sorry about that," he said. "My sister's a little, uh, tactless."

"That's okay. I like your family. They remind me of one of those families on television shows. You know, the happy kind."

David's expression became gentle. "Yeah. They're all right," he said. "I'll go get the debate notes, okay?"

Lindsay nodded and he left the room. It had been a long time since she'd been around an entire family other than the Golds. It felt nice.

"How does this debate work, anyway?" she asked David when he came back. "I've never seen one before. Except for a Presidential one, on TV."

"It's basically the same principle," David answered. "One side makes an opening statement. Then the other side makes theirs. While they speak, we prepare our rebuttal. We note down the major points being made, and go through our cards, picking out the statements that best argue against what they're saying. Both teams go back and forth like that. At the end the judge decides which team has scored the most points."

He looked down at his notecards. "Maybe we

ought to let what's-his-name, Ron, make the opening statement."

"But he hasn't even worked with us," Lindsay objected. "I'd be surprised if he even remembers what the topic is."

"Yeah, but I don't trust him to give a rebuttal," David said. "If we let him have the opening statement, I can just write it out for him. Then all he'll have to do is read it. He won't have to think." He paused. "Guys like that really get on my nerves. He doesn't care about this at all. Like he said, he's only doing it to get extracurricular activity for his college applications."

"David, I don't know why I'm telling you this, but that's the only reason I joined the debate team, too."

"Yeah, I sort of figured that. But at least you've put some real work into it. Ron hasn't. He's probably never had to work for anything in his whole life."

She waited for him to add 'like most Benedict kids.' When he didn't, she was pleasantly surprised.

For the next hour the two of them pored over their notes, discussing, organizing, and numbering them. Finally David gathered up all the index cards and put them in a little cardbox. "I think we're ready. Good work, partner." Gravely he shook her hand. He glanced at his watch. "If you want, we can make that movie. I told Pete and Connie we'd meet them at the theater if we finished in time."

"Great!" Lindsay said. Afraid she sounded too

excited, she added quickly, "I've been wanting to see that film."

"Oh, yeah?" David got up. "What's playing?"

"Um, I forgot."

David grinned. "Yeah, I've been wanting to see that one, too."

There was a line in front of the movie theater. Lindsay spotted Connie as they crossed the street. A tall, thin boy stood with her.

Connie made the introductions. "Pete goes to Madison," she said. "I keep telling him he's smart enough to get into Benedict, but he says he's happy where he is."

"You don't have to be so smart to get into Benedict anyway," Lindsay said. "I'm there, and believe me, I'm no genius."

"You have to be smart if you want a scholarship," Pete told her. "At least, you have to score pretty high on the exams."

Lindsay was puzzled. "What exam? I didn't have to take any exam."

"Of course you didn't," David said. "You had the money for tuition."

His tone was nonchalant, but Lindsay felt embarrassed. "Well, that's not my fault," she said.

"Certainly not," Connie said gaily. "We don't blame you for it! We'd all like to have your money!"

Her frankness was disarming. Lindsay found herself laughing along with the rest of them.

In the theater they all got popcorn and sodas and settled down in seats toward the back. It was a good movie, a comedy about an inept bank robber. At one point Lindsay was laughing so hard she wasn't even aware of the fact that David had taken her hand. By the end of the movie it felt so natural, she felt she could have gone on holding hands with him forever.

After the movie they went across the street to an ice cream shop. They settled down at a table by the window.

"That was great!" Connie said. "The scene where he hands the teller the wrong note was hysterical." They all went over their favorite scenes. For the first time in ages Lindsay felt totally, happily, relaxed.

"What time is your debate on Monday?" Connie asked Lindsay. "I want to come and be your cheerleader."

Lindsay giggled at the image of Connie jumping up and down and cheering in favor of capital punishment. "You mean, something like 'kill 'em, kill 'em, rah, rah, rah'?"

"Hey, not bad," David said. "It's creepy to be arguing in favor of killing people, though. I almost hope we lose. I haven't found one argument that convinces me capital punishment is right."

"I know," Lindsay said. "The more I learn about it, the more it seems wrong." She turned to Connie. "The debate's at three-fifteen, after school on Monday."

"Why don't you join the Debate Club?" Pete asked Connie. "You love to argue."

Connie laughed. "Only with you! Besides, in a debate you have to be objective and unemotional, right?"

"Absolutely," David replied.

"Forget it," Pete said. "When Connie argues, she screams and cries and goes totally berserk."

"That's a total lie!" Connie yelled, punching him on the shoulder. "I need to do something, though. I did try to join the Benedict League, but they didn't let me in."

Lindsay suddenly became very interested in spooning up the hot fudge sauce that had dripped down to the bottom of her sundae. She could feel David's eyes on her, and she knew she had to say something.

"I just joined the Benedict League. Maybe if you apply again—"

"Why should she?" Pete interrupted harshly. "Your club already made it pretty clear what they think of scholarship girls like Connie."

"Pete!" Connie punched his arm again. "Don't talk like that. I know some of those girls are snobs. But some of them must be okay. Look at Lindsay. She's a member! And she doesn't seem like that at all!"

"Thanks," Lindsay said.

"And besides," David said, "the question of whether or not she likes scholarship girls is not the question uppermost in *my* mind. I'm more concerned with whether or not she likes scholarship boys."

Lindsay looked up at him, startled. But Connie went on as if David had just said the most casual thing in the world. "Anyway," she said, "I don't think the Benedict League is right for me. I get enough teasing from my neighborhood friends about going to a fancy private school. If they knew I was in an exclusive club like that, I'd never hear the end of it. Of course, when they find out the playground's going to be torn down, they're really going to come down on me."

"But don't you think it will be nice for us to have a swimming pool?" Lindsay asked.

"Nice for us," Connie said. "Sure. Who wouldn't want a swimming pool?"

"But think of what it's going to mean for the neighborhood," Pete said. "No place for kids to play. I realize it's on private land, but for years people have thought of that playground as public property. Losing it is really going to upset people. Especially since it's being replaced by a pool only kids who go to Benedict can use."

He looked at Lindsay as if he was expecting her to argue with him. She just stared at him blankly. She didn't really have a single argument against what he was saying. It *wasn't* fair to the neighborhood. But was not being able to build the pool fair to Benedict?

Connie broke the silence. "The problem with the pool is out of our hands," she said. "I need you guys to help me with *my* problem. Think of something I can join. I don't care about the Benedict League. But I need to find some sort of extracurricular activity for my college applications!"

Lindsay couldn't help it. She started to giggle. David looked at her. And suddenly both of them were laughing.

"Hey!" Connie exclaimed. "What's so funny?"

David's eyes didn't leave Lindsay's as he answered her. "Private joke."

12

"**N**ERVOUS?" DAVID ASKED.

"A little," Lindsay admitted.

They were alone in the classroom where the debate was to be held. Two tables had been set up in the front of the room. There were three chairs at each, with a podium between them.

"There's nothing to worry about," David reassured her. "The judge will be sitting over there. But you don't have to look at him when you're speaking. Just look straight ahead."

"Right at the audience?"

"What audience?" David asked. "Connie will come and probably a couple of others. Maybe somebody from the school paper. But that'll be it."

Lindsay hid a smile. He was in for a real surprise. The Bennies would just about fill the room.

David put the box of note cards on one of the tables and set out a couple of legal pads. "I saw your aunt's article in *Saturday Magazine*."

"Uh-huh."

"I thought it was great. Did you read it?"

"Yes. Do you have an extra pen or pencil?"

"Just one. Don't you have one?"

"I forgot."

"You're obviously not a professional debater yet, Ms. Crawford. I'll go to the office and get you one."

"Thanks."

He ran out of the classroom. Lindsay breathed a sigh of relief. She couldn't face talking about Margaret's article—not yet.

Early Saturday morning she'd gone out and picked up the magazine at a newsstand. She'd taken it to a coffee shop—not Luigi's, but another one, where she was sure she wouldn't run into anyone she knew. Over two cups of tea she'd carefully read her aunt's article from beginning to end.

Margaret could really write. The article was lively, gripping, and disturbing. Lindsay was particularly impressed with Margaret's description of the playground. Somehow, with words alone, Margaret was able to capture the life of the playground so that Lindsay almost felt as if she was there.

Margaret's plea for the playground was passionate, but the article didn't attack Benedict Academy. It was more like a gentle reprimand and a reminder of how much the playground meant to the neighborhood.

Lindsay pulled her thoughts back to the present and flipped through the note cards on the desk. *Too bad Margaret isn't on our debate team*, she thought. *She has the gift of persuasion.*

David returned with a handful of newly sharpened pencils. Right behind him were Karen and the boys from the other team. They were followed by Mr. Roberts, the history teacher, who would be judging the debate.

A couple of students Lindsay didn't know came in and took seats in the back. Then Connie ran in. She took a seat right at the front.

"Where's Ron?" David whispered. "He should be here by now."

"I have no idea." She was busy watching the door. She saw Jennifer come in, followed by Margaret.

Lindsay was stunned. She hadn't even invited her aunt to come to the debate.

"Hey, we've got five whole people in the audience," David murmured. "That's some kind of record."

"We'll get more," Lindsay promised, glancing at the door again.

David was watching the door, too. He looked relieved when Ron finally sauntered in.

"Here," David said. "You're going to read this. It's our opening statement." He handed Ron a typed sheet.

"No sweat," Ron replied. "Then can I leave?"

"No," David said flatly. "You have to sit there until the debate's over."

Ron heaved a sigh. Mr. Roberts rapped on the podium; it was time to begin.

Lindsay looked at the door in bewilderment. She had given the Bennies the day, time, and place—more than once.

She sat down next to David. He gave her hand a quick squeeze under the table.

"You okay?"

"Okay."

"Go," David ordered Ron.

"Resolved: That capital punishment should be a mandatory sentence for first-degree murder," Ron read aloud from the podium. He looked at the audience and grinned foolishly. "Hey, I'll buy that."

"Just read," David whispered.

Ron wasn't exactly a great speaker. He fumbled over half the words and generally made it obvious that he had no idea what he was saying. Despite his poor performance, Lindsay was impressed with the speech David had written for him. It was intelligent and logical and carried a strong message. Lindsay wondered how David could write so convincingly about something he didn't even believe in.

When Karen presented the other team's opening statement, Lindsay listened carefully. She jotted down each point the girl made. At the same time, she and David flipped through their cards, rapidly locating the statements that would counter her remarks.

When Karen finished, David reached under the table and gave Lindsay's hand another quick squeeze. As Lindsay approached the podium, she felt almost confident.

Keeping her voice steady, she presented her arguments, one by one.

When she'd finished she was startled to hear someone clapping. She looked up. Margaret put her hand to her mouth, as if she'd suddenly realized clapping wasn't appropriate. Lindsay flushed, but

she couldn't help smiling. It was the kind of spon-
taneous gesture her mother might have made.

The next person on the other team spoke. Lindsay had to admit he made a solid attack on her
argument. Then it was David's turn.

He was awesome. Unless you knew his real feelings about the subject, as Lindsay did, you'd believe he was an ardent proponent of capital
punishment. *He'll be a great lawyer someday*,
Lindsay thought.

But it wasn't just his performance that was making her heartbeat quicken. That funny tingle she'd
been getting every time she was with him was be-
coming more intense. She'd never felt that way
about a guy before, not Parker, not anyone. *Lindsay Crawford, she told herself, you're in love*.

She felt like throwing her arms around David
when he returned to the table. It wasn't easy to
concentrate on the final speaker from the other
side, though he was good, too. Not as strong a
speaker as David, maybe, but he had impressive
facts and figures to counter everything David had
said. All loyalties aside, Lindsay knew the other
side had the better argument.

She wasn't surprised when Mr. Roberts announced his decision. She just hoped David
wouldn't take it too hard. To her surprise, he didn't
appear disturbed at all.

"You really can't expect to win when you're arguing in favor of something that's morally wrong,"
he said philosophically.

"You've got strong convictions, David," Lindsay
said.

"I'll bet you do, too."

Do I? Lindsay wondered.

"Hey, is this going to look bad on my record?" Ron asked anxiously.

"It's just the participation that you put on your college application," David told him. "Admissions people don't care if you win or lose a debate."

"Whew," Ron said. "See ya!"

Connie, Margaret, and Jennifer surrounded the debate table. "You guys were great!" Connie said.

"Yeah. You practically made me change my mind about capital punishment," Jennifer added.

"You did a fine job," Margaret said.

"I was surprised you came," Lindsay said. Margaret's smile faded a little. "I mean, I'm glad," Lindsay added. "I just didn't expect you."

"I was going to suggest a little celebration," Margaret said tentatively. "I realize we can't have a victory celebration, but maybe we can have a consolation one."

"That sounds good to me," David announced. "After all, this was a victory of sorts—a moral victory, anyway. I gave this my best shot, and I still couldn't convince the judge that capital punishment is right."

"Good point," Lindsay said.

"*You* were fantastic," David told her. "Especially considering this was your first debate."

"You really were," Margaret agreed. "I had no idea you had a talent for this."

"Neither did I," Lindsay said. For a moment, their eyes met. *Maybe we just need to get to know each other better,* Lindsay thought.

"Let's go," Jennifer cried. "I'm starving."

"It's my treat," Margaret said. "How does pizza sound?"

There was unanimous approval.

They walked to the pizza place just a block from Benedict. As they looked over the menu, Connie turned to Margaret. "Are you the Margaret Crawford who wrote that article in *Saturday Magazine*?"

"Guilty," Margaret said. She seemed to be avoiding Lindsay's eyes.

"That was a fantastic article!" Connie said.

"Thank you," Margaret said. "How does everyone feel about mushrooms?"

"I couldn't put it down," Connie continued.

"Neither could I," Lindsay said. Margaret turned to her. "You read it?"

Lindsay nodded. The happiness in her aunt's face gave her a peculiar pain.

The waitress appeared, and they ordered a large, pepperoni–mushroom pizza with extra cheese.

"You really got to the heart of the matter," Jennifer told Margaret. "A private pool versus a public playground."

"That's pretty much what it boils down to," David said. "Unfortunately, I don't see how everyone can possibly end up happy."

They all started talking at once, but Lindsay couldn't concentrate on what they were saying. Jennifer's words kept reverberating in her ears. Private pool, public playground. Private pool, public playground.

"What?" Margaret asked.

Lindsay hadn't even realized she'd spoken out loud. But she repeated the words. "Public pool."

"What are you talking about?" Jennifer asked.

"That's it! That's what could solve this whole thing!" Lindsay exclaimed.

"What?" David asked.

"We could have the pool. After school hours, and in the summer, it could be open to the neighborhood. It doesn't have to be a gigantic pool, either. There could be space for a wading pool for the little kids, and maybe even a sandbox and some other playground equipment. Not as much as there is now, of course, but some."

"Lin," Jennifer said, "that's a brilliant idea!"

"And no one would mind giving up some playground space if they had a pool," Connie added.

"Lindsay, you're a genius!" David said. "I can't wait to see you get up at the meeting tomorrow night and present the idea."

"Me? I was thinking . . ." she turned toward Margaret. "Maybe you'd like to suggest it."

"Me? Why?" Margaret asked.

"Well, I'm not really comfortable speaking in front of people. . . ."

"You were just fine today," Connie pointed out.

"It's your idea," Jennifer said. "And you should get the credit for it."

David turned to her. "Lindsay, are you worried that certain people won't like finding out it's your idea?"

That was exactly what she was afraid of. If she stood up and presented her idea, the Bennies would probably never talk to her again.

"Lindsay." Margaret's voice was soft. "If you don't want to speak at the meeting, I will."

Lindsay could feel David watching her. "Thanks a lot, Margaret. I just don't know yet."

"I checked a video out of the store today," Margaret said to Lindsay when they got home. "Want to watch it?"

"Okay," Lindsay answered. "But I think I'll get out of my uniform first."

Lindsay went to her room, pulled off her clothes, and put on a long nightgown. One of her slippers lay on the floor, but its mate was missing. She got down on her hands and knees and peered under the bed. She spotted the slipper and reached out to grab it. Her fingers touched something else, something small and metallic. She picked it up.

It was an earring. Lindsay stared at the small gold disc with the tiny dangling amethyst. At first it didn't look familiar. Then, with a rush, she recognized it.

It had been her mother's. The week before her parents left, Lindsay had begged to borrow the pair. She couldn't remember the occasion, but she was wearing her violet silk blouse, and the amethyst earrings matched perfectly.

The next morning, when her mother asked for them back, Lindsay could find only one on her nightstand. They were one of her mother's favorite pairs, a gift from Lindsay's father before they were married. Together they'd looked all over Lindsay's room, but they couldn't find the earring anywhere.

And now here it was. Lindsay held it up to the light to watch the gem sparkle.

"Lindsay?" Margaret was in the doorway. "Why are you sitting on the floor? What's wrong?" Her aunt came in and knelt on the floor next to her.

"My mother's earring. I found it."

Margaret touched her shoulder, and Lindsay started to cry.

Suddenly she found herself wrapped in Margaret's arms.

"I miss her," Lindsay sobbed. "And my father. I miss them so much."

"I know, I know," her aunt murmured, stroking her hair. "Oh, Lindsay, I'm so sorry."

"Sorry for what?"

"Sorry that they died. Sorry that I haven't been much of a substitute."

"No one can be a substitute," Lindsay said.

"Yes, I know that. But I haven't really been here for you, have I?"

"What do you mean?"

"Oh, Lindsay, I knew I couldn't be a mother for you. But I didn't know what to be. I don't know what you want me to be."

"I don't know what I want you to be, either."

Margaret was silent. The unsettled, confused look on her face was strangely familiar to Lindsay. Then she understood. It reflected everything she'd been feeling herself.

"I care about you, Lindsay. Maybe you don't know that. But I do. It's just that I've been so afraid. . . ."

"Afraid?"

"Of trespassing. Of intruding where I didn't belong. I didn't want to come on like a parent from out of nowhere. You know, asking questions, making rules. I didn't think you'd want that."

"You were right," Lindsay said.

"So I held back. It meant less friction, I guess, but it also meant I didn't become part of your life. It was as if we were roommates—strangers. And now—" she paused. "Lindsay, what do you want me to be?"

"I don't know," Lindsay replied slowly. "You can't be like my mother . . . or my father."

"Of course not. I could be a good friend, I think."

Lindsay's voice was barely a whisper. "I think I want you to be more than that."

"What do you want me to be?" Margaret repeated.

"Family," Lindsay whispered. Why had it been so hard to admit? Now Lindsay knew. Because it meant finally admitting that her other family was really gone. Irrevocably gone, forever and ever.

13

AT BREAKFAST THE NEXT MORNING, LINDSAY SAT QUIetly across the kitchen table from her aunt. Margaret was quiet, too. Lindsay felt awkward, as if they were meeting for the first time. In a way, they *were*. At least, Lindsay felt she was looking at her aunt with new eyes.

Margaret cleared her throat. "Tonight's the big meeting," she said at last.

"Mmm. It'll be interesting to hear what people have to say."

"I can't wait to hear their reaction to your idea," Margaret said. "How did you come up with that, anyway?"

"I'm not sure," Lindsay replied. "In a way I was inspired by your article. Honestly, Margaret, I had no idea you were such a good writer."

"Thanks."

"I guess there's a lot I don't know about you."

There was a moment of silence.

"So are you going to get up at the meeting to-night and present your idea?" Margaret asked.

"Yes." Lindsay hoped her voice carried more conviction than she felt.

Her aunt reached out and touched her hand. "You've got guts. More than I knew you had. I guess there's a lot I don't know about you, too."

Lindsay was still a little nervous about the Bennies. But the more she thought about it, the more obvious it seemed. The Bennies couldn't possibly object to a reasonable, fair solution that let them keep the pool without taking anything away from the kids who used the playground.

There was a knock on the door. Lindsay jumped up to get it.

"Jennifer!"

"Hi. Ready for school?"

It was like old times. "See you later," Lindsay told her aunt. Impulsively she kissed Margaret on the cheek.

"Wow!" Jennifer said as they left the apartment. "Things sure have changed around here."

"They really have," Lindsay said. She told Jennifer about her conversation with Margaret the night before.

"That's great, Lindsay! And I'm really excited about your idea for the playground. When you didn't sign our petition, I was shocked."

"I just had to make up my own mind about it," Lindsay said. "We've got a Benedict League meeting right after school. I'm going to tell them my idea. Maybe they'll go along with it."

"You really think they'll like it?"

"Why not? It's a brilliant idea. You said so yourself."

"Yes, but I don't know if the Benedict League will think so."

"You sound just like David. You assume because they're Bennies they're going to be snobs about this. You've got to open your mind."

"Since when did you become so broad-minded yourself?"

"Well, I'm trying. I guess David's had a lot to do with it. He's made me aware of things I never thought about before. Not that he can't be pretty narrow-minded sometimes. I think maybe I'm helping him see things differently, too."

"Sounds like the beginning of a beautiful relationship," Jennifer teased.

"Jen, I hope so."

When they entered the school, Claire ran to meet them. "Hi, Lindsay!" she said, ignoring Jennifer. "Don't forget about the Benedict League meeting right after school. It's in the student lounge."

"Okay. I hope I've got a better memory than you have!" Lindsay said lightly.

"What do you mean?" Claire asked.

"My debate yesterday!"

"I'm so sorry," Claire cried. "It completely slipped my mind. How did it go?"

"They did a fantastic job," Jennifer interjected.

"But we lost," Lindsay added.

"Oh, too bad. By the way, I read your aunt's article in *Saturday*."

"Yeah? What did you think of it?"

"Well, everyone's entitled to her own opinion, I guess. See you later!"

Jennifer turned to Lindsay. "Still think you're going to get their support?"

Lindsay gazed at Claire's departing figure. "She hasn't heard my idea yet. Besides, Claire's not the whole group."

By the time Lindsay left her last class, she was pretty nervous. What if the Bennies didn't support her idea? Would she still have the guts to present it to the whole school?

As she reached her locker, her face broke into a smile.

"David!"

"Hi, genius," he greeted her. "Ready for the big meeting tonight?"

Lindsay nodded. "I'm going to meet with the Benedict League now and tell them my idea."

David's smile vanished. "They're not going to like it."

"What makes you so sure?"

"Because they're snobs. And they're not going to like the idea of ordinary people swimming in the same water they swim in."

"David, sometimes I think you're the snob! You can't make broad assumptions like that!"

"Oh, yeah?"

She faced him. "What did you think of me the first time we met?"

"I thought you were a typical Benedict snob."

"And what do you think of me now?"

He didn't answer right away. When he spoke,

his voice was low. "I think you're someone I could fall in love with."

Lindsay felt as if she and David were somehow encased in their own private bubble. All around them students were running up and down the hall, slamming locker doors, yelling and calling to each other, but they seemed far away.

Then the bubble popped. Jennifer came running up, looking frantic. "You guys aren't going to believe this."

"What?" Lindsay asked.

"The president of the student council was supposed to moderate the meeting tonight. But he's got the flu! And now Mr. Hanson says *I* have to moderate it."

"You'll be terrific," Lindsay said.

"That's right," David agreed. "But you might want to bring some bodyguards. Just in case...."

"Don't worry," Lindsay said to Jennifer. "No one's going to attack you."

"Yeah," David said. "I'll tell my buddies not to throw rocks or nuttin'."

"Thanks a lot, buddy," Jennifer said.

"I'm late," Lindsay said. "I've got to run to the Benedict League meeting. Listen, you guys, let's all meet at my place and go to the meeting together. That way, if Jennifer starts to freak out, we can drag her up to the podium!"

David reached out and lightly ruffled her hair. "Sure thing."

When Lindsay entered the student lounge, at least twenty Bennies were there. But they were all gathering their coats and books.

"You're late," Claire said sternly. "The meeting's over."

Lindsay glanced up at the clock. "You mean the meeting only lasted ten minutes?"

"I had our statement already prepared, and we approved it." She handed a sheet of paper to Lindsay.

Lindsay glanced at it. It was just what Claire had said at lunch the other day: Benedict was a private institution with no obligation to provide a playground for the neighborhood.

"Wait a minute!" Lindsay called to the girls heading toward the door. "I want to tell you guys about an idea I had."

Everyone turned to look at her.

"We could open the swimming pool to the public when school wasn't in session. That way we'd get our pool, but the people in the neighborhood wouldn't be losing everything."

Several girls appeared interested, but then they all turned back to look at Claire, who was still standing at the back of the room.

"Did your aunt put you up to this?" Claire asked Lindsay coldly.

"No! It's my idea."

"I see. Well, it won't work."

"Why not? I know there are a lot of details that would have to be worked out. But there's definitely enough space there, and I'm sure if Benedict set up a committee—"

Claire didn't let her finish. "Lindsay, this is a chance to have our own private pool. It would be like a country club attached to the school! You don't let just anyone into a country club."

"But what about—"

"Lindsay, we've got our statement, and I'm going to present it tonight as the official position of the Benedict League. Like I told you, Bennies stick together."

Lindsay looked at the girls clustered around the door. None of them returned her gaze.

Claire flashed her a brilliant smile. "Listen, Lindsay. You're a new Bennie, and I think it's just great that you want to share your ideas with us. But we're all in agreement on this. See you tonight!"

14

"**O**H, NO," JENNIFER MOANED. "LOOK! MY PARENTS are sitting right up front."

"My mom's up there, too," David said. "Dad stayed home to watch Sally." Lindsay spotted Connie Velez sitting next to Mrs. Jeffries.

"We'll sit up front, too," Margaret told Jennifer. "That way you'll see a lot of smiling faces."

"Thanks," Jennifer mumbled, but she didn't move.

"Am I going to have to drag you up there?" David asked her.

Jennifer squared her shoulders and started up the aisle.

Watching her, Lindsay's own fears began to creep back. Was she really going to present her idea? She had to. She couldn't disappoint Margaret or Jennifer. Or David.

Then she saw the Bennies all sitting together in the middle of the auditorium. Looking away, she started down the aisle with Margaret and David.

"Hey, Lindsay!" Claire called to her. "We're over here!"

It was noisy in the auditorium and easy for Lindsay to pretend she didn't hear. But when they reached the front row, she saw that there were only two empty seats left.

"You guys sit together here, and I'll find another place," Margaret offered.

"No," Lindsay said. "You guys stay here." She turned and went back up the aisle.

She greeted the Bennies and slipped into the seat they'd saved for her.

A head in front of her turned around. "Hiya, babe."

"Hi, Parker." She managed a smile. He smiled back. Well, at least she knew she hadn't broken his heart.

The principal rose and opened the meeting: "The donor is an avid swimmer. He specified that the money be used for a swimming pool. It cannot be used for any other purpose. A committee from the student council has requested this meeting to discuss the implications of building this pool. Now, I'd like to introduce Jennifer Gold, vice president of the student council, who will tell you the committee's concerns."

Jennifer stood up and began her speech.

At first her voice quavered, but soon it became strong and confident. "We're concerned because building this pool will mean destroying the playground that now occupies that land. We think that since many people in this community make use of that playground, we should hear how they feel about this. The floor is open to discussion."

A well-dressed woman rose. "I don't see why this meeting is necessary. It's Benedict's land and Benedict's money. Any decision to be made should be made by Benedict Academy."

There was a smattering of applause. Then David's mother rose. "That's true, but the playground has been very much appreciated by the community. There are no other public playgrounds close by. It would be a real loss to the neighborhood if it has to be torn down."

This was greeted by applause, too. Then Jennifer's mother got up. "I'm very troubled by this. On the one hand, I like the idea of Benedict having a swimming pool. I think it would be wonderful for the students. But on the other hand, that playground has benefited the school as well."

"How?" a man in the back called out. "It's a children's playground. Benedict students don't use it."

Mrs. Gold went on. "If any of you read Margaret Crawford's article in *Saturday*, you know what I mean. That playground has helped to cement good feelings between Benedict and the community. I'm afraid that the loss of the playground will create hostility."

The room began to buzz with voices. Jennifer stepped forward. "Please," she said. "If you have something to say, stand up and share it with all of us."

Lindsay tensed. Was this the right time for her to talk?

Before she could get up, Claire rose from her seat. "As president of the Benedict League, a service organization that works to support Benedict Academy, I have a statement on behalf of our group."

Despite everything, Lindsay couldn't help admiring Claire's self-confidence. Claire had charisma and a manner that demanded respect.

I don't have any of those things, Lindsay thought. *How can I possibly speak after her?* But then she started listening to what Claire was actually saying.

Claire's statement sounded good, but it said nothing new and offered no solution. It was like Claire herself, all style, no substance.

Claire sat down to polite applause. Then Lindsay stood up. She didn't have to look to know that all the Bennies were staring at her. Maybe she was committing social suicide, but she knew she couldn't live with herself if she didn't speak up.

"I'd like to present a possible compromise to this problem." She was shaking, but she forced herself to go on.

"There's enough space in the playground area for a pool *and* a smaller play area. I realize the pool couldn't be as big as some people might like, but we don't really need a huge one. The pool could be used by the students during school hours, and be open to the community after school and during vacations."

When she finished everyone started talking at once. Lindsay couldn't make out exactly what anyone was saying. She saw Jennifer grinning at her from the stage.

Mr. Hanson cleared his throat. "That's a very interesting possibility," he said. "I propose that we create a committee made up of students, parents, and community members to look into it."

The audience burst into applause. Lindsay sank back down in her seat. It had worked. Everyone liked her idea. Well, almost everyone.

Claire was glaring at her.

Parker turned around. "You know, you're getting pretty weird."

"Maybe I like being weird."

Lindsay looked around at the other Bennies. Some were staring at her, others at Claire. She couldn't tell what they were thinking.

"Thank you all for attending," Jennifer said from the stage. "Anyone interested should come up and sign this sheet. We'll put you on a mailing list to keep you informed about this issue."

People were getting up, milling around, and talking. Lindsay didn't wait to hear the Benedict League verdict on her action. Instead, she jumped out of her seat and hurried to the front. As she passed Jennifer's parents, they both gave her a thumbs-up sign. David's mother beamed and waved.

"You did that beautifully! Lindsay, I'm so proud of you," Margaret said.

"Thanks, Aunt Margaret," Lindsay answered. Her aunt's eyes widened. Lindsay realized it was the first time she'd ever called her that.

Margaret was the first to throw her arms around

her, then Jennifer, Jennifer's parents, Connie Velez
. . . and finally David. He hugged her so tight she
could barely breathe.

"I suppose the Benedict League will kick you out
now. Do you care?"

Before Lindsay could answer, Sheryl from the
Benedict League and another Bennie came up to
her. Lindsay eyed them apprehensively. They were
probably bringing a message from Claire.

"That was a great idea," Sheryl said.

"But—you heard me telling Claire about it at the
meeting this afternoon. Why didn't you say anything then?"

Both girls looked embarrassed. "Well, it's kind
of hard to argue with Claire," Sheryl said. "She's
got this thing about how Bennies stick together."

"How we're supposed to be like a family," the
other girl added.

"But families argue," Lindsay pointed out.

"Yeah," Sheryl said. "But try telling that to
Claire. See you later, Lindsay."

Lindsay turned to David. "See?" she said.
"They're not all snobs."

"Maybe not," he relented. "But it seems to me
that they're all under Claire's thumb."

Lindsay shrugged. Maybe they were, but they
could change. It was all a question of attitude.

"Forget Claire, let's get something to eat," David
suggested.

"I'm too beat," Jennifer said. "I think I'll just go
home with my parents and let them tell me how
wonderful I was."

"How about you, Connie?" Lindsay asked.

Connie grinned. "When was the last time you two had any time alone?"

Lindsay smiled gratefully.

"I'm going straight home and to bed," Margaret announced. "I have to get up early tomorrow." She kissed Lindsay's forehead lightly. "Now don't stay out too late. It's a school night."

"C'mon," David said. "I'm starving."

Together they walked out of the auditorium. It was a beautiful night.

"Star light, star bright, first star I see tonight, I wish I may, I wish I might . . ."

"What are you going to wish for?" David asked.

Lindsay thought it over. Weeks ago, there was so much she could have wished for.

"I don't know. I feel like I've got everything I want. You can have my wish."

"But I've got everything I want, too."

"Oh, c'mon," Lindsay teased. "There's got to be something. You don't want to waste the first star."

"Okay." He closed his eyes.

When he opened them, Lindsay asked, "What did you wish?"

He put his hands on her shoulders and gazed at her seriously. "I wished for . . . a bacon-double-cheeseburger and a side of fries."

Lindsay smiled thinly. "*That's* what you wished for?"

"Actually, I made two wishes. I wished for a cheeseburger and a side of fries. And you . . . loving me."

"Um, your first wish is available at the coffee shop around the corner."

But as he pulled Lindsay toward him and lifted her face to meet his, David didn't seem to be in a great rush to get his first wish after all.

About the Author

Marilyn Kaye is the author of more than 30 books for children and young adults. She gets many of her favorite story ideas from her own vivid memories of friends, family, school, home and growing up. Marilyn is a professor at St. John's University. She lives and writes in Brooklyn, New York.